MY SUNSHINE

Having escaped a controlling relationship, won the lottery and given up work, Jenny is adrift at twenty-nine. Then her landlady's widowed son Alexander seeks her help in a family emergency, and she is catapulted into a different world of muddy boots, wayward pets and three children in need of love and a firm hand. But Jenny is conflicted — to fall for Alexander means absorbing so much responsibility, and then there's his obvious uneasiness when it comes to her fortune. More importantly, do Alexander's feelings match her growing love for him?

Books by Anne Holman
in the Linford Romance Library:

ANNE HOLMAN

MY SUNSHINE

Complete and Unabridged

LINFORD
Leicester

First published in Great Britain in 2019

First Linford Edition
published 2020

A catalogue record for this book is available
from the British Library.

ISBN 978–1–4448–4428–3

Published by
Ulverscroft Limited
Anstey, Leicestershire

Set by Words & Graphics Ltd.
Anstey, Leicestershire
Printed and bound in Great Britain by
T. J. International Ltd., Padstow, Cornwall

This book is printed on acid-free paper

1

London, 2015

Winning a fortune isn't much fun! Miss Jennifer Warner hadn't gone to the cinema that rainy afternoon because she hadn't wanted to see the film anyway — she simply wanted to avoid feeling lonely.

She smiled wryly as she walked out into the busy street where crowds of people pushed by her with their bulging shopping bags, thinking, *If my former workmates knew how I felt now, they might laugh!*

Why? Because Jenny had left work after winning the National Lottery! Yes — earlier that year, everyone's dream to win a fortune had come true for her when all her numbers had come up.

At first, after Jenny had been told how much she had won, she felt gobsmacked. Her head was spinning.

People crowded around to congratulate her on her good luck.

Then she tried to pretend it hadn't happened — she wanted her life to go on as normal.

But it didn't work out. Her friends at work remained her friends, but some were envious of her good fortune — and others wanted her manager's job.

Jenny, you don't need to work any more! People kept telling her. Or, as Jenny felt, they kept nudging her to leave.

Eventually she left her job, thinking that whether she liked it or not, she'd been given the chance to start a new life.

At the age of twenty-nine, she had a lot of time to think about her future.

Her mother had died when she was young; her diplomat father worked abroad and was rarely in touch. With no brothers or sisters, she was completely on her own.

It was challenging at first, finding a

new place to live in a posh neighbourhood, then more enjoyable shopping to her heart's content to fill her new flat with whatever took her fancy.

Then as the months went by, her friends gradually lost touch with her. Jenny hadn't thought about the fact that her new address wasn't near them, or that the office chat she was used to hearing had become less interesting as she wasn't there any more.

She'd begun to going to the cinema some afternoons when she wasn't taking classes: learning to drive, cookery, pottery, learning Chinese and going to the gym.

However the gym had been a disaster because she'd injured her knee on some apparatus — and all the sports physio could suggest was that she needed a new knee!

Jenny was glad to escape from the gloomy atmosphere of the cinema. She hadn't enjoyed the film, and her knee ached. Having to walk the short distance back to her flat was quite pleasant, though, as the early evening sunshine had replaced the afternoon rain.

Leaving the busy shopping mall, she walked by the noisy traffic on the main road towards the quiet, fashionable avenue where her new flat was.

Suddenly she became aware of someone shouting behind her.

Always a little nervous of being on her own in London, with the news headlines telling everyone that crime was on the increase, she limped on.

'Oi, lady!'

The sound of running footsteps behind her made Jenny stop and press herself up against a low garden wall so that the jogger, or whoever it was, could race by. Maybe she was in the way on the pavement.

But the footsteps slowed, and a panting male voice sounded close as he huffed, 'You left your umbrella behind in the cinema.'

Jenny's mouth fell open. She had taken her umbrella to the cinema and walked out without it!

Turning to see the man who'd come to return it to her, her eyes widened on seeing a tall, good-looking young man holding out her red and blue owl-patterned umbrella.

'Thank you,' she mouthed, almost afraid to say the words because you never knew with lone men. She wasn't far from her flat, but she couldn't walk fast with her sore leg — and he could run.

His keen eyes were assessing her. She decided he didn't look as though he was about to attack her, and was more inclined to add him to the list of unattainable men she'd seen or fancied over the years: film stars, sports stars, married men . . .

After accepting her item of lost property, she was amazed when he sat down on the low garden wall to recover from his sprint. His thick, dark hair flopped down, making Jenny think he should have gone for a haircut instead of going to the cinema. His athletic body fitted his quality suit nicely, and his shiny shoes kicked against the wall as though he didn't care whether the heels got scuffed.

'Do you live around here?' he asked.

His direct manner made Jenny squirm. What was it to him if she did?

However, she didn't want him to think she might be waiting for a bus, as they were not far from a bus stop.

'Further up the road,' she found herself saying, waving in the direction she was heading for.

His sharp blue eyes penetrated hers as he enquired, 'What number?'

Alarmed once more, Jenny licked her lips and said nothing.

His face broke into a smile — ever such a nice smile as he seemed to guess why she appeared nervous. He turned his face away so as not to embarrass her further.

'Don't worry.' Even his deep voice sounded reassuring, 'It's just that my mother lives down this avenue. Number 146.'

Jenny gulped. That was the number of the house where she had her flat! His mother must be her landlady, Mrs Sharman, who Jenny liked — although she hadn't known her for long.

Number 146 was a grand Victorian-built town house. It had been the Sharman family home for donkey's years and when Mrs Sharman had become a widow, she'd decided not to downsize but to take in a tenant to live upstairs — and that was herself.

Feeling she didn't have to mistrust him any longer, Jenny said, 'That's where I live.'

He slipped off the walk and shook her hand firmly as though they were being properly introduced. 'Ah — hello, Miss Warner. Mum told me a charming young lady had taken the flat upstairs. My name is Alexander.'

'I'm Jenny. Pleased to meet you.'

His manners were old-fashioned, and she liked that. And he was taller than she was — a bonus, as she was considered tall for a woman.

In fact, she thoroughly approved of her landlady's son — what she'd seen of him so far.

Jenny fidgeted. Her leg had begun to ache.

'I must get going,' she said. 'I've hurt my knee and it's telling me I ought to get back and rest it.'

'You could come and sit here on the wall for a minute or two. It's quite warm in the sunshine.'

Jenny hesitated. Then she decided, *Why not?* and sat down beside him.

He said, 'I'm waiting for my son, William. He has a football practice after school this evening.'

So he was married. Jenny wasn't surprised. He was such a handsome man — just the kind she'd been hoping to meet some day. But someone had beaten her to it.

It was pleasant, sitting on the wall with him in the warm sunshine. It was companionship. Just what she wanted.

'Meow!'

Suddenly a sleek, creamy-coloured

Siamese cat, with beautiful blue eyes and chocolate ears and tail, sprang up on the wall and made Jenny jump. Then she recognised it was Mrs Sharman's cat and gave the animal a stroke.

She said, 'Your mother's cat, Belle, has come to share the sunshine with us.'

'Actually, Belle is my cat. Mum is looking after her for me, until I get things settled.'

'Oh?'

He turned his head to look at her, seeming unsure of whether to explain his situation. But she sensed he was not going to enlighten her, as he stroked his cat and sighed heavily.

Several reasons flooded into her mind. Was he having trouble with his work — or his family? She shouldn't pry, as it was none of her business.

They smiled thinly at each other. They both had problems.

'Well, I must struggle on,' Jenny said, slipping off the wall. Using her umbrella as a walking stick she began to tread along the pavement.

'Do you mind if I come with you?' he called.

Stopping, she turned and replied, 'If you wish.' It wasn't the most enthusiastic invitation, but then she didn't want to sound as if she cared whether he walked with her or not.

Actually, she felt thrilled to bits. Walking down the avenue with a confident, professional man was her dream come true. Having a fortune in the bank seemed to her insignificant compared to having a desirable man by her side!

He couldn't offer to take her arm because he held the cat, which was occasionally protesting loudly, but it wasn't necessary. He didn't question her about herself, although his initial friendliness indicated he may have liked to know more about her. And she dare not try to breach the barrier of privacy he had obviously built around himself.

A rather sad young man, she decided

he must be. Was his marriage an unhappy one?

Arriving at the house, Jenny went up to the front door and, taking the key from her handbag, unlocked it.

Old but elegant, Mrs Sharman stood in the hall beaming to see her son.

'I was sitting by the front window and saw you coming. I'm glad you've met. And you have found Belle, too!'

Feeling she didn't want to intrude on the family reunion, Jenny made for the staircase saying, 'I must rest my leg.' Painfully she clambered up the stairs, glancing back to see Alexander disappearing with his mother into her downstairs flat.

For some reason, Jenny felt herself ecstatic. She unlocked her front door, went into her luxury apartment and sighed. Dropping her handbag on the nearest chair and shrugging off her raincoat, she went to put the kettle on in her shiny, spacious kitchen. She liked a clean kitchen; her new light wood units were as immaculate as when they had just been fitted, even though she enjoyed cooking and had been using the appliances regularly.

Having made the tea, she took a hot mug of it into her sitting room. She flopped into a comfortable armchair near her front window, then sipped it appreciatively.

Looking out of the window, in the room which had once been the master bedroom of the house, she began to relax — and ponder.

Mmm. Alexander! That was a nice name, it suited him.

Why couldn't he have turned up at one of her classes? A man looking for a partner like her? But he was married, and she wasn't the kind of woman who would want to take a man away from his family — or become his mistress ... What was she thinking! She shook herself.

No, she had to make more effort to get out and about and meet more men who were available — though she doubted whether she would ever meet anyone she would take such an instant instinctive liking to as she had Alexander Sharman.

Well, she certainly wouldn't meet any suitable candidates sitting here dreaming about attractive men like him!

Recovering her normal good humour, Jenny decided to prepare a casserole for her evening meal. She would make enough for three or four meals and freeze the other portions. She had some fresh braising steak and vegetables in the fridge, as she'd been out shopping earlier that day.

Meals at expensive restaurants were nice — and there were many places she could go to eat in the neighbourhood — but there was nothing quite as tasty as home cooking.

Turning on a music station on the radio, she was soon chopping and slicing onions, carrots and turnips and preparing a beef stock as she hummed merrily.

* * *

The early evening news had just begun on the TV when Jenny became aware of an urgent rapping on her front door.

Putting down her glossy magazine, she frowned. Who on earth could that be?

Opening the door, she was astonished to see Alexander Sharman. And even more surprised to see the apologetic look on his face.

'Miss Warner — ' his voice so husky it made her wonder if he had a cold as he cleared his throat and began again, 'Miss Warner, I'm so sorry to trouble you but my mother suggested you might be willing to help me.'

The mention of his mother made Jenny relax into a warm smile.

'How can I help you?'

'I have a problem,' he said — unnecessarily, as Jenny had already surmised the poor chap might have several. She wasn't averse to listening to tales of woe and helping people if she could.

'Won't you come in?' She stepped

14

aside. A cup of tea and a chat with him would be lovely, and allow him time to express his concerns.

He shook his head saying, 'I'm in a hurry and need to borrow your car. Urgently.'

Jenny blinked. She'd bought herself a top range sports car because she was talked into it by an expert salesman. It was true she wanted a car — she had just passed her driving test — but a little hatchback would have been fine as she was toying with the idea of getting a dog. The most expensive sports model on the market wasn't on her shopping list, and she couldn't believe how reckless she'd been in buying it. But in a weak moment she had done, and there it was in Mrs Sharman's garage. A sleek sports car waiting to go out for a run.

Not for a moment did she hesitate. She felt certain Alexander was a good driver, and he would return the vehicle in pristine condition. It wasn't as if she needed to use it at present. Anyway, by the anguish on his face he appeared to be in dire need of a car.

'Sure. I'll get the car keys.'

Off she darted and was back in no time, offering them to him.

'You'd better get your raincoat and hat. It's raining heavily.'

Eh?

'I don't want to go for a drive this evening, thanks.' Jenny sounded decisive. She'd thought of going to bed early.

'You've got to drive.' His statement was as definite as hers had been.

She took a deep breath.

'Mr Sharman — I can't drive it.'

He looked cross.

'Mum said you were taking driving lessons.'

'True. But I've only just passed my test!'

He gulped. 'I will help you — guide you.'

Jenny held out her car keys.

'Look, Mr Sharman. The garage key is on the ring. Take them and don't

16

worry about using my car — it needs a run.'

He had eased himself into her flat and kicked the door behind him so that it closed with a click.

Jenny gulped. Feeling uneasy, but not afraid, she stepped back.

'Mr Sharman!'

'Alexander.'

'Very well, Alexander. I'm not telling you I am unable to drive because I don't want to help you. It's because I have never driven my car. But you are very welcome to use it.'

He blinked. 'Miss Warner — '

'Jenny.'

'Right, Jenny. I should explain. My son, William, is twelve, and has not come back from school after football practice. He usually walks back here and stays with his granny until I fetch him after work and bring him home.'

Jenny detected the quaver in his voice and a glistening in his eyes.

'I'm really worried about him. I don't know where he is . . . he has a mobile

17

phone but he hasn't called me. It's Friday, the rush hour, and I can't wait around for a taxi. I need a car to go out and start looking for him now. It's getting dark.'

Jenny put her hands over her mouth, sharing his fear for his son. London was a huge place — even the area where she lived. And the light was fading fast.

Alexander looked at her pleadingly as he went on to explain further.

'William's been upset since his mother died a few months ago, and he may have gone to friends instead of coming here. I just don't know. He should have rung me — or his grandmother.'

Jenny felt a lump in her throat. No wonder he was distraught! He was newly bereaved.

She dragged her attention back to the present as he continued, 'My car was taken for its MOT and replacement parts this afternoon. It is still in the garage, because they rang to say it won't be ready to collect until tomorrow.

'That's why I need to use your car. So can you come with me? Please?'

2

Jenny felt as though someone had punched her. Shaken, she tried to absorb the shocking news.

Taking a deep breath, she made herself stay calm. Then summoning courage, she said calmly, 'I'm truly sorry to hear about your wife's death — ' She closed her eyes. That was not the reason he was here. Although not having a wife must add to his responsibilities, his pressing need was to locate his boy. London was a huge city with many dangers.

Suddenly, to her great relief, her practical manager's nature kicked in.

'I'll certainly allow you to use my car. But as I said, I'm still a very new driver. And I've had hardly any experience of driving at night. Nor have I ever driven my new car. I've always used the instructor's.'

He cleared his throat.

'I'll be with you. You'll be fine as long as you are accompanied by an experienced driver. Which I am.' He squared his wide shoulders as though he, too, wanted to shake off his cares for the present and deal with the urgent matter that confronted him.

'Jenny, I could call a friend or even my brother — or a taxi — but it may take time before anyone else is able to help me find William. So I must beg you to come with me. I'll be in the car with you, directing you as though I'm a driving instructor. I can not only tell you where to go, but can keep my eyes open for spotting William.'

This was a practical plan of action — an immediate way of dealing with the problem.

Only Jenny felt paralysed with fear. Afraid to use her beautiful new car she had never driven. She'd always used the driving instructor's vehicle. Oh God! She hadn't even read the BMW instruction manual — only glanced through it. She wasn't sure what she had to do to get the engine started! Although it had an automatic gearbox, she was aware of dozens of knobs and dials. She didn't know how to switch them on and off — or what they might do if she did!

Feeling sweat prickling on her brow, Jenny wondered if it was right for her to venture out on the road in a powerful, unfamiliar car at all, let alone in the dark and at rush hour.

Yet she had passed her test, at the first attempt, and her instructor constantly went over the instructions in the Highway Code. He'd got her to drive not only in the quiet back streets but also through busier parts of town, even a couple of times on a dual carriageway, and given her practice in the usual manoeuvres.

So she wasn't exactly unable to drive, was she? Just unsure of her ability — that was what was making her quake.

Alexander seemed quite certain he

could act as her instructor. She wouldn't be surprised if he was an expert driver. She certainly didn't think he'd be a bad one.

'Let's get going, then!'

Through her anxious daze she became aware that he had stepped up to the coat rack and was taking her mac off its peg, offering to help her put it on.

Now was not the time to protest. It was the time for her to overcome her reluctance. She would have to take the plunge and drive her car before long — and this was effectively an extra lesson she was having, she told herself.

'Please hurry!' he yelled from outside her front door as she fetched her handbag.

Yes, I must be brave. Conquer my fear. Trust Alexander, who needs me to help him find his boy.

She gathered her wits enough to grab the magnetic P-plates from the hall table before she followed him out of her flat and downstairs — not even stopping to lock her front door.

Downstairs, Mrs Sharman was waiting by the front door and opened it for them.

'Thank you, my dear,' she said to Jenny. 'I'll stay by the phone in case William rings, and then I can call you on your mobile if he does. Or if he turns up. Now do take care — it's a wet, stormy night.'

Alexander swore as Belle darted by him and out into the garden as he was opening the door for Jenny.

'We can't wait while we find the cat. She'll find somewhere to hide.'

He knew where the garage was because he'd been brought up in this house. He was familiar with the rusty locks and knew the trick to open the old wooden doors smoothly.

'Wow!' he exclaimed as he saw the superb new sports car parked inside. 'Mmm. I like your choice of wheels.'

Jenny wished she'd bought herself an old banger instead of this bright red monster that should be still in a showroom.

'Alexander . . . won't you drive? I'm frightened!'

He ignored her plea, took the P-plates from her shaking hands and fixed them on the car, back and front. Then unlocking the driver's door, he held it open for her to get in.

'Don't be worried, Jenny. I'm teaching William to drive at an old airfield, so I'm perfectly confident I can guide you. You'll be quite safe in this beautiful new car — it will frighten every other car on the road when they see it coming!'

Recognising his effort to lighten her mood to give her confidence, Jenny looked up at his steady smile. Catching a glimpse of pain and worry in his eyes, she forced herself to lift her lips into a brave smile. He was under stress and making the effort to overcome his fears, and so must she! She'd done nothing much to help others since she'd left work. Now was her chance to do a good turn for someone, although it was difficult for her.

She slid into in the driving seat and Alexander adjusted her seat belt. He asked her to check the driving mirror and made sure her seat was comfortable for the pedals.

Dashing around to the passenger door, he opened it, plonked himself down beside her and clicked his own seat belt into place, saying, 'The smell of new leather is wonderful! Now let's see if it works!'

Without her having to ask him, Alexander began to instruct her what to do, and the engine began to purr. He showed her how the wipers worked, and where to switch on the headlights.

'Now put the gear lever into reverse . . . ' He went on to tell her exactly what to do, step by step, as through her panic she began to remember herself how it was done.

Soon they had backed out of the garage, turned to face the road, and the car slid out of the front drive into the empty street.

It was a great deal different from the instructor's old car she was used to driving.

Her new car was magic. A smooth, gliding ride.

I'm enjoying this! she thought.

But before long they ended their run along the quiet avenue and turned onto the busy main street. Now she had to concentrate hard on her driving, and she knew Alexander's eyes were darting everywhere, looking for his boy while directing her where to go, which lane she should take and reminding her about traffic lights and indicating they were turning onto another road.

'I'm taking you to William's school, which isn't far, a few more minutes. I hope he may be waiting for me to pick him up — although I told him to walk back to his grandmother's house and wait for me there.'

Jenny was thankful to know they hadn't far to go. His instructions were clearly stated, which gave her confidence.

'There's the school ahead. Go into the grounds and park in one of the teachers' parking spaces.'

She did so. It wasn't difficult because there were very few cars parked there.

Nor was there any sign of children.

Alexander was out of the car like a shot. He ran towards the school, barging through the double doors. After a while he came out just as quickly and hurried back towards Jenny's car.

Panting, he blurted out, 'I saw the caretaker, who told me all the football players left the school a couple of hours ago. He took me to the games changing rooms but there was no sign of William or his kit.' He ran a hand distractedly through his hair. 'He is in the process of sweeping the classrooms and saw no sign of any boys in the building.'

'Oh, dear! So now what?'

Alexander's hand rubbed over his weary face.

'He could have gone home with his friend, Paul. He lives near. I ought to contact him. Paul may have some idea where he is.'

'Do you have his phone number?'

'No. We'll just have to go there and ask Paul. Fortunately, I've often driven William to his home — so I know how to get there.'

Jenny didn't argue. How could she? This situation was becoming serious. Her heart bled for Alexander. How he must be suffering.

Following his precise instructions, they were soon out in the midst of the Friday rush hour traffic once again. Although the rain had lessened, it was still necessary to use the windscreen wipers and headlights and Jenny's pulse was pounding with the effort needed to keep going.

* * *

Finally, after a prolonged tour around a housing estate, they found Paul's house. His parents, and their son, were dismayed to hear that William hadn't returned to his grandmother's house as he usually did after school.

'They have no idea where William is,' reported back Alexander after talking to the family. 'They are going to ring the police for me. They think I should report him missing. I think we should go back to Mum's house now and wait for news.'

Jenny didn't attempt to talk. She just followed the instructions he gave her to get back to his mother's home.

Cars and vans rushed by her. The noise of the traffic was intimidating, and now car lights flashed in her face. But she was determined to obey Alexander's orders and ignore his increasing tetchiness as he found it more difficult to direct her. A van driver swerved dangerously in front of them. Alexander leaned over to press the horn while Jenny clutched the driving wheel and trembled.

Knowing she had an important job to do, she battled on even though she felt the pain in her leg becoming worse. It was a nightmare! A car hooted at her for changing lanes, and a huge lorry almost took her side mirror off.

At last, they reached a quieter road with houses on either side.

A blast of a police siren made her wobble as it swept up alongside and passed her. She slowed, indicated and came to a stop at the side of the road. Oh, Lord! Had she violated a traffic rule. Would she get a penalty?

An officer rose out of the police car and, putting on his cap, came striding towards her. She quaked. She'd never been in trouble with the police before and this officer looked grim-faced.

But Alexander was out of the car and striding to meet him. The police officer who was driving the squad car came to join them too. They stood talking for some time.

Jenny began to realise that she was not at fault. Alexander was telling them about the lost boy. One officer, she noticed, was a woman and she was taking notes.

Able to relax a little, Jenny decided to get out of her car and stretch her sore leg.

Ouch! It was agony. She made the effort to walk along the pavement a little way.

Then, to her amazement, she saw Belle! The blue-eyed Siamese was there, trotting along a side road.

Immediately Jenny was concerned that the cat might get run over and hobbled after it, thinking she should catch it.

But Belle was off again, running away from her down another road and making towards a small figure, which the cat circled around.

Jenny blinked. A miracle had occurred before her eyes!

Belle had shown her where Alexander's son, William, was!

Emotion overwhelmed her. Tears rolled down her cheeks. Crying out and waving, she hobbled back to the wider road and soon the police officers and Alexander had hurried up to meet her and were listening intently, trying to make sense of her sobbing.

'I've seen William!' She gave a gulp. 'At least, I think it's him — back there on that side street.' She pointed to the corner she'd just walked around. Then, taking a deep breath, she added more calmly, 'His cat, Belle, showed me where he was.'

The men ran to find the missing boy.

The next thing Jenny knew was that the policewoman had placed her arm around her.

'It's OK. His father is with the boy now. We must get you home.'

Jenny glimpsed Alexander ushering the boy — and the cat — into the police car and they drove off immediately.

Aghast at seeing Alexander leaving her, Jenny exclaimed, 'This is my car, but I'm only a new driver — I don't think I can drive it now!'

The policewoman shook her head.

'No, I don't think you should. You've had a shock. I'll drive your car home for you. What is your address?'

There were lights on in the hall when Jenny arrived.

The policewoman had driven her car back apparently effortlessly and parked it in the garage as confidently as if it were her own. She locked the garage doors and gave the keys to Jenny before ushering her into the house.

There, Jenny observed pandemonium. So much noise, with everyone talking. Mrs Sharman was hugging William, who unsurprisingly was soaked, but also looked as if he'd been kicked about like a football. Alexander was talking to the policeman, while the cat was yowling for her dinner.

Jenny thanked the policewoman and hobbled upstairs, leaving the family reunion to calm down.

Jenny had barely had the time to shake off her shoes, hang up her raincoat and handbag, when there was a knock on the door.

'Come in,' she called, her sore leg

34

refusing to take another step as she sank down on her sofa.

In marched Alexander. His previously haggard face was alight with joy.

With no more ado he came straight up to her and taking her hand, kissed it, then her flamed cheek.

'I can't thank you enough!' he whispered.

His wide smile was catching, and Jenny smiled up at him. But she didn't want his praise or thanks — she wanted to know how William was.

'It was Belle, the cat, who found him.'

'Yes — but you found them both!'

He sat down beside her on the sofa and explained, 'All I know at present is that William got lost on his way here.'

'I don't understand. Your son walks here every day after school, doesn't he?'

Alexander nodded.

'From what he told me, I understand some older boys from another school bullied him. They punched him because he wouldn't give them his mobile. They took away his school bag and threw it over a wall, so he lost all his things — including his mobile which he'd put in his bag.

'They frightened him so much that he decided to walk another way here — and got lost. He was wandering around for hours in the rain. Then Belle appeared and he tried to get her to lead him here . . . he's very fond of his mother's cat.'

'How is William? Is he badly injured?'

'Sore, hungry and angry, but he'll survive.'

There were so many questions Jenny longed to ask him. But it wasn't the time. Both Alexander and his son needed a good meal and a rest — as she did.

'Has Mrs Sharman got a hot meal for him? I have a beef hotpot in the oven you may like to share with me.'

Alexander's eyes shone as he rose straight away.

'Brilliant! Mum hasn't much more than the sandwich he normally has when he comes home from school. Then I usually run him back to our cottage to have dinner with my other children.'

His other children! Jenny blinked.

'Who's looking after them now?'

'Polly's parents. Their other grandparents . . . ' But Alexander's mind was clearly focused on his hungry son and he was already at her front door, opening it and calling back, 'Is it OK if I bring William up for your meal?'

'Yes,' she said uncertainly. Would she have enough for them to eat?

He left immediately.

Groaning with pain, Jenny got up and hobbled to the kitchen. But she had no time to feel sorry for herself as she began making some small dumplings to add to the beef casserole pan. Then she took out two packets of creamed potato from the freezer and put them into the microwave.

By the time she'd laid the table, she heard a tap on her front door and called, 'Come in.'

Alexander ushered in his freckled, bruised-faced son, who had obviously had a bath since his ordeal as his face was clean, his ginger hair tidy and he wore pyjamas.

'William is ashamed of his battered face,' whispered Alexander. 'He wouldn't have come up, only he says he's famished — and Granny only has some biscuits downstairs.'

Jenny smiled at the scowling boy and said smartly, 'Sit down at the table and I'll serve you before you die of hunger. Where is Mrs Sharman?'

Alexander explained that his mother always ate her main meal at midday and only liked a snack in the evening. She was looking after the cat.

The casserole was delicious, having been cooked for several hours on a very low heat. Tender chunks of meat, soft root vegetables and herby dumplings were covered in a tasty gravy. Her guests ate every scrap of the food, and when William lifted his plate to lick it clean, Alexander shouted at him, 'Put your plate down, William!'

Jenny said calmly, 'I expect you've got room for a dessert, William — so there's no need to eat my plate!'

At her words, William's face broke into a smile.

'What have you got?'

'Let me see . . . ' Jenny thought wildly. 'I made a chocolate sponge cake the other day.'

'Yes please,' William said remembering his manners.

'With a scoop of ice cream, perhaps?'

William nodded.

'With lots of ice cream, please, Miss Warner.'

'Shall I make some coffee?' asked Alexander, who had regretfully declined the cake and was eyeing the sloppy chocolate mess his son had mashed together and was enjoying. Jenny was relieved to rest her knee while he put on her kettle and found the coffee.

It soon became clear that William was having difficulty staying awake.

As she sipped her coffee, Jenny

turned to ask Alexander, 'You're not going home tonight, are you?'

'Nope. My car is still in the garage being repaired and won't be ready until midday tomorrow, so I'll sleep on Mum's sofa. William can have her spare room — he does occasionally spend the night here with her.'

Jenny looked at the exhausted man. She felt sad to think him having no proper bed to sleep on. He needed a comfortable night after his ordeal.

'I have a spare room too,' she said. 'I suggest you sleep downstairs with your mum. William can use my spare room. He's almost asleep — and he's too big for you to carry downstairs.'

Alexander ruffled his son's bright hair.

'Don't do that, Dad! I'm not a dog!'

No, thought Jenny, smiling — *he's more like an angry tiger cub!*

Alexander sighed and whispered to her from behind his hand. 'I won't inflict him on you, Jenny. His behaviour can be difficult to manage.'

From what little she'd seen of him, Jenny felt sure young William was no worse than many of his age growing into manhood. She smiled kindly at the boy and said, 'You've had a rough time today, William, and I think you'll find my new spare room memory-foam mattress very comfortable. The bed is made up, so if you'd like to sleep there overnight you're very welcome.'

William gave a grunt, but it was clear to Jenny that if he didn't lie down soon he would fall over. She put her arm around his thin shoulders and guided him to the spare room, showing him where the light switches were and turning down the bedclothes.

He sat on the bed as if to test the mattress by bouncing up and down, then lay down saying, 'Yeah, it'll do . . .' and immediately fell asleep.

Jenny gazed with sympathy at the boy's bruised face and swollen eye. Acute sympathy for him brought tears to her eyes. He'd just lost his mother, and he'd suffered being bullied and had run off and lost his way home. Poor little chap!

Patting her eyes dry, she switched off the bedroom light and returned to the kitchen to find Alexander busy washing the dishes.

'Stop that!' she cried. 'You need to go to bed — you've had a harrowing evening.'

'So have you!'

'I suppose.'

She had to agree as her leg was throbbing with pain.

He said, 'It was a delicious meal — thank you.'

'It was just ordinary grub. But you were hungry so you appreciated it more. Now, off you go downstairs.'

She seized the drying cloth he was holding and pushed him towards her front door.

He stopped before opening the door and, bending down, he kissed her lightly on her cheek.

'Thank you, Jenny. You're a beam of sunshine!'

As he left, clattering down the wooden stairs, she smiled at the unusual nickname he had given her.

She also felt warm inside to know she had made herself useful. She felt valued. She'd survived some hair-raising experiences tonight — but she certainly didn't feel lonely any more!

3

Jenny awoke next morning when she heard her doorbell ring.

Who the hell is that? If it's the postman, he'll just have to leave whatever he's brought me outside.

She then tried to move and smothered a scream.

My bloody leg is agony! Yesterday's fun and games have crippled me!

The bell sounded again — this time more insistently.

Daylight was streaming in through her bedroom windows — she hadn't pulled her curtains last night as she'd fallen exhausted onto her bed.

Her bedside clock showed it was eight o'clock.

Go away!

But whoever it was didn't go away.

Then they came into her flat! Thud, thud, thud, the heavy footsteps sounded along the hallway.

Was she dreaming?

Thinking it must be Alexander, Jenny grabbed her robe and was just tying up the strings, wincing with every movement, when there was a knock on her bedroom door.

'Come in!' she called cautiously.

She half expected it would be Alexander bringing her a cup of tea. What she didn't expect was to see a tall, slightly grey-haired man, very like Alexander, but far more confident-looking.

He barely smiled at her as he stood by the door and said in a voice very like Alexander's, 'Good morning, Miss Warner. I've come to see the patients.'

Closing her gaping mouth, and gathering her wits, Jenny managed to croak, 'William is in the spare room down the corridor.'

'I've checked on him. He's still sleeping, and it's best to let the boy rest.'

Lord! He's coming over towards me!

45

'Who are you?' she squeaked.

He looked surprised as he glared down at her.

'I'm James Sharman, a private orthopaedic surgeon.'

'Oh!'

'Didn't my mother tell you about me?'

Jenny didn't like to say she hadn't. There was something that warned her she should have known. He was bursting with self-importance. Evidently he was used to bossing around young doctors and nursing staff.

'I've come to examine your knee, Miss Warner. Alexander told me you'd injured it and it was causing you great pain.'

That she couldn't deny.

'I gave it a hard time yesterday,' she said, wanting to tuck the injured leg under her duvet.

He knelt on the floor by her bed and said imperiously, 'Let me see it.'

Well, she could hardly refuse such a command!

46

He was surprisingly gentle the way he lifted her leg and examined it, ignoring her yelps of pain.

'You'll need a complete knee replacement,' he declared. 'I'll send around a nurse tomorrow for your pre-op tests and X-rays.'

Jenny gasped. 'Oh no, you won't!'

He seemed not to hear her protest, as he left her bedroom as swiftly as he'd come in.

Jenny heard his heavy footsteps thud their way out of her flat and the front door click shut.

Stunned, she retreated under the covers, pulled her duvet up to her chin and stared at the ceiling.

Did I dream that?

★　★　★

Hours later she was woken once more, by a tap on her bedroom door. Then it came again, as if the person outside was impatient.

Swinging her legs out of bed, and

yelping as her knee objected, Jenny hobbled to the door thankful she still had her dressing gown on.

Tousled-haired, fresh-faced, William stood outside looking up at her enquiringly.

'Do you do breakfast?'

Grinning at his cheek, Jenny replied, 'I do. What do you like?'

He grinned back at her. 'On a Saturday, Dad cooks us bacon and eggs, fried bread and tomatoes — and if he has them, mushrooms and sausages too.'

Mmm! Jenny thought that sounded good!

She cleared her throat. 'Well, If I go to the trouble to cook you all that, I expect you to get washed and dressed first.'

'But I haven't any clothes to get dressed in.'

A male voice sounded from somewhere in the flat.

'Yes, you have, William. I went out early and did some shopping and I've got you some new underwear, jeans and a jersey from Marks and Spencer.'

My goodness! Alexander had obviously bought some bacon too, as Jenny could smell it sizzling in the pan. He was cooking the breakfast!

Should she really be surprised at that? If he had lost his wife, then he would have had to take over all the domestic chores.

William shouted back, 'Dad! I'm not wearing Marks and Spencer jeans. I want Levis.'

Jenny could hear Alexander shouting at him.

She put her head around the door and said sharply, 'William. You're not having any breakfast if you don't get yourself dressed in the clothes your father has kindly bought for you. You know your school clothes were in a dreadful state last night and your grandmother is probably washing them ready for school next week.

'Now I'm going to have a quick shower, and I suggest you do too or . . . '

She didn't hear any more protest from the boy as he sped off to do as he was told.

She'd never had such a quick shower in her life, and with her painful leg it made the process worse. But slipping on clothes and brushing her hair she managed, although she thanked God for her naturally curly brown hair, and good complexion that didn't require more than a lick of lipstick.

By the time she arrived at the kitchen, father and son were already relishing their full English breakfast.

Alexander got up immediately on seeing her, and giving her a wide smile said, 'Good morning.' Then he pulled out a kitchen chair for her. Using a folded cloth he took a plate from the oven and placed it in front of her: a perfectly cooked golden egg, crispy bacon rashers, sausages, a triangle of browned fried bread and a halved tomato.

'Sorry, no mushrooms were available in the market this morning,' he said.

'We live in the country and collect wild mushrooms from the nearby fields. Now, would you like tea or coffee to drink, Jenny?'

'There's no orange juice either,' commented William with his mouth full.

He ducked in time as his father made to slap him playfully.

Jenny smiled. 'I'd love a cup of tea. But after you've finished your breakfast.'

'I'll make you some tea, Miss Warner,' offered William, quickly gobbling up what was left on his plate. Surprisingly the boy was soon up on his feet filling the kettle and asking, 'Where do you keep the tea bags?'

His father winked at Jenny — rather proudly, she thought. The boy could be courteous when he chose to be. But Jenny was aware he could be a handful too.

Jenny thoroughly enjoyed her breakfast — and the cup of tea William made and carefully poured out for her.

Alexander waited until his son had gone downstairs to see his grandmother and Belle, whom the boy seemed to be fond of, before he commented, 'I hear you had a visitor early this morning.'

Jenny nodded, raising her eyebrows.

'My flat has become as busy as a railway station recently — people coming and going — '

'Jim says you'll need a new knee and has offered to do the operation for you.'

She made no comment as she watched him get up and pour them both a second cup of tea. He sat down near her again as he went on, 'Jim works for a private hospital. You can have the operation done privately and straight away, to get you out of pain.'

Jenny said with the same stubborn voice William used to annoy his father, 'I don't want to have an operation, thank you.'

'Oh, but you do!'

Jenny knew he was right. But what he didn't know was that medical matters terrified her. Way back in her childhood she remembered being given horrid-tasting medicines, having painful injections and being made to wear braces on her teeth. She was determined not to go through anything like that again!

He buttered a piece of toast as he continued, 'Jim is my brother. A top orthopaedic surgeon. You don't have to take my word for it. Look him up on your computer.'

Crashing her cup down on her saucer, Jenny said, 'I dare say he is!'

'He reckons your knee op should be straightforward surgery. You'll be walking around with no pain in a matter of weeks.'

'Does he now?'

Alexander's large hand came up and landed tenderly over hers and she looked up, startled, straight into his piercing blue eyes.

'Believe me, Jenny, I only want to help you — do you a good turn. You were wonderful yesterday helping me to find William. Now I want to repay you.'

She stiffened, but didn't feel like pulling her hand away.

'I don't need your help, thank you.'

'Yes, you do. You need a new knee, urgently. Jim was quite certain about that. He's a very busy surgeon, but he's willing to fit you onto his list in the next few days.'

When his great paw gave her slender hand a slight squeeze, Jenny pulled her hand away from under his and stood up — making a face with the pain that shot though her knee as she did so.

Turning her face away from him, Jenny said curtly, 'Please tell your brother I really appreciate his offer. But no. No, thank you. I hope I have made that clear.' She drew in a long breath and gave a weary sigh. Then as if to cast off her decision about that problem she said cheerfully, 'Now hadn't you better go and collect your car from the garage?'

Alexander shook his head as he rose and looking at his watch said, 'Yes, I'd better. I'm sorry to leave you with the cleaning up, but I ought to go and collect my car and get home before my in-laws murder my children.'

Jenny thought, *How many has he got? And are they all as difficult as William?* But she didn't like to delay him by asking those questions. She was just glad he had something else to think about other than her sore knee!

Leaving abruptly, she thought he blew her a kiss as he disappeared into the hallway and let himself out of the front door.

* ⋆ ⋆ ⋆ *

Left to tidy up the kitchen, rinse the breakfast things and put them into the dishwasher, she found it impossible to cast him from her mind. But she told herself all that had happened yesterday was over and done with, and she could go back to living her quiet life. She might not see him again — or just catch a glimpse of him when he visited his mother.

After bundling the spare room bed linen and towels into the washing machine, Jenny was glad to take the newspaper and settle down on the sofa for a rest with a cup of coffee. She tried to put Alexander out of her mind. His problems were his problems — not hers!

However, the newspaper fell into her lap as she recalled the sensation of his warm hand covering hers which had been so comforting, and his blue eyes, she remembered, looked beautiful. Caring. She tried to identify the spell he was casting on her, pinking her complexion.

Perhaps I'm falling in love with this guy!

She'd certainly never felt quite like it with any man she'd known before. Not even the man she had almost married — years ago — who'd left her to marry one of her friends.

That had been a terrible experience too.

Marvin had been a manipulator. But,

because she was still a teenager and flattered by his amorous attentions, she didn't see him like that when she became engaged to him. Like the big brother she didn't have, he'd told her what to do all the time. Then she realised Marvin was making every decision for her.

She wasn't having any more of that! If Alexander was thinking he could dominate her life — even if she liked him — he was very much mistaken.

As the day wore on, she had to admit she might be able to overcome her tendency to keep thinking about the previous evening's adventure — but not the painful throbbing in her leg that even strong painkillers couldn't shift.

She wondered if she should go downstairs and see Mrs Sharman, but she couldn't face going up and down the staircase.

Tomorrow was Sunday and she might make the effort.

She lay in bed thinking sadly that she'd have to look for a new flat

— somewhere on the ground floor. How could she manage the stairs any more? It would be such a shame to have to move from this lovely apartment, arranged just as she wanted it.

She would lose touch with Alexander Sharman too . . . and that was a pity.

★ ★ ★

Sunday seemed a long day. Missing the excitement the Sharman family had given her, Jenny tried to rest her leg and catch up on a few friends by phone and email.

Wishing Alexander would ring, she decided he must be far too busy to be thinking about her as she was thinking about him.

She searched online for a ground floor flat but didn't see one that she would be seriously interested in — or maybe she just didn't want to find one. She wasn't in the mood to go house-hunting.

4

Monday morning at last! Jenny's bedside radio showed the clock hands at nine-thirty.

Heavens that's late! At least I slept well.

Swinging her legs out of bed, Jenny hoped the night's sleep had cured all her troubles. But — ouch! It hadn't. The action of moving her injured knee caused her to gasp.

Gingerly, she proceeded to get up.

After a shower and dressing, she was drinking her morning cup of tea when she heard the doorbell ring. Hoping it might be Alexander, she hobbled to the door.

Outside stood a large, dark-faced woman in uniform, with a warm smile. Jenny thought she must be a police-woman, coming for a statement about William being missing on Friday.

59

'Hello, Miss Warner. My name is Sister Mary. Professor Sharman sent me to chat to you about your knee operation. And take some samples.'

Open-mouthed, Jenny stepped back as Sister Mary walked in carrying a bulging black bag. She plonked down her bag and calmly removed her navy jacket, revealing her nurse's uniform.

Catching her breath as her old fears kicked in, Jenny said sharply, 'I told Dr Sharman — '

A brown hand appeared in front of Jenny's face as if to stem her words.

'OK, I know what you told him.' This experienced nurse was obviously expecting Jenny to protest. She said cheerfully, 'Before you say any more — pop the kettle on, will you? I've been on duty all night and I'd love a cup of tea. And it's *Mr* Sharman — he's a surgeon.'

Flabbergasted, Jenny tried to find her voice. But she thought she shouldn't refuse a hard-working nurse a cup of tea, especially as she'd been up looking after patients all night.

She ushered her visitor into her kitchen and put the kettle on. The only thing she managed to stutter was, 'Would you like a piece of toast? I was about to make some for my own breakfast.'

Mary's smile melted Jenny's feeling of hostility towards the visitor. In fact, Jenny warmed to her friendliness and her willingness to call in on her, as she'd obviously been asked to do, although she was tired after her long shift and probably would prefer to go home. Only Mr Sharman, in his domineering way, had told her to call on Miss Warner and she had no choice but to come.

They helped each other to prepare the breakfast and drank the teapot dry as they sat at the kitchen table and munched the toast, happily chatting about anything from the weather to the latest soap on TV.

As Jenny hobbled to the sink with the dirty dishes, Mary delved into her capacious bag and withdrew some packages which she laid on the cleared kitchen table.

Jenny swung around.

'Stop!' she shouted. 'I told Mr Sharman, and his brother, that I am not having surgery.'

'I know, Mr Sharman told me you were quite definite about that.'

'So why are you here?'

Mary chuckled. 'It doesn't take a surgeon to see that the way you walk shows you really need to get that leg of yours fixed!'

'That's no concern of yours. Nor Mr Sharman — or anyone else for that matter.'

Mary answered calmly, 'People trained in orthopaedics know the agony people can suffer if they are unfortunate and injure their hip or knee. I see patients every day whose life is ruined by their disability and they beg us to treat them. Some are old, some are young with a sports injury such as I understand you suffer from. If nothing is done, they become permanently lame.

'Now Mr Sharman doesn't want that to happen to you. Nor does he like to see you in pain. That is why he is offering to replace your knee. Now don't say that it won't affect your life if you don't have it done — it will. Now sit down so I can take your bloods.'

A wave of revulsion came over Jenny. *Bloods!* Even the word gave her the shudders.

Her mind also registered the fear she had of needles.

The thought of her skin being punctured was enough to make her wish she could run away out of the flat — but of course she couldn't. She could just about hobble. And if she did, where would she go?

This is a nightmare! And who is to blame for it? Alexander Sharman! How dare he start running her life — it was just like Marvin's manipulative behaviour all over again.

Also, because of her sore knee, the

thought of having to look for a new place to live upset her.

I like it here! I really don't want to move. Moisture welled in her eyes.

I've got this flat just as I like it, with new furnishings, and painted in the colours I chose. Lovely fabrics for curtains, carpets and bed linen. And kitchen units . . . How will I manage, trailing around looking at new apartments with my painful knee? Then having to move all the new stuff I've bought. And will I ever drive a car again?

To her horror Jenny found tears trickling down her face, which she wiped off savagely. But it was no use. Overcome with the realisation of her bad luck, she collapsed on a kitchen chair, put her arms on the table so that she could lean forward and rest her aching head, and began to sob.

Pent-up feelings of anger washed over her, with added feelings of hopelessness — what on earth had happened to her normal cheerful self?

She had all the money she could ever want. All the free time to do as she liked — and a gammy leg, an accident, had spoilt it all for her.

How she wished she hadn't won a fortune. She would much prefer being an ordinary working girl again with normal pain free knees.

Mary gently put her arm around Jenny's shoulders. Her reassuring nurse's voice said softly, 'No one is going to make you do anything. We're not allowed to do any treatment without your consent.'

Jenny continued to sob. Mary sat by her patiently, combing her hair back from her distressed face.

'It's going to be all right. That's why Mr Sharman sent me, to tell you everything is going to be all right. It's been a nasty shock for you. But you haven't got to make up your mind this minute. I'll go away now if you like — but you'll regret it as you'll probably decide you do want some help before long. And then you might not get the best surgeon like Mr Sharman, and you may have to wait for ages for an operation.'

As Mary passed her a bunch of paper tissues to pat her eyes, Jenny thought about it.

Why would Sister Mary lie to her? Neither she nor Mr Sharman were looking for work — they both sounded overworked.

Then part of the truth came into her mind.

'I can't stand injections!' she blurted out.

'Heavens, how many have you had? You don't have diabetes, do you?'

'No. I remember having a painful one as a child at school.'

It sounded very much as though Mary gave a chuckle.

'Good gracious, that must be twenty-odd years ago, girl! Now you won't feel more than a slight prick.'

Shuddering, as she endeavoured to gain her self-control, Jenny mumbled, 'Call me a coward.'

Sister Mary exclaimed, 'No. You're not! No one chooses to have an accident — or to have an operation, for that matter. But sometimes it's necessary. Doctors and nurses care about their patients. They offer to give the best treatment they can to make a person better. It may not be pleasant for the patient, but today we are able to provide powerful painkillers — and operations like new hips and knees are commonplace and successful.'

Jenny squeezed her eyes shut. Sister Mary had been sent to her to explain the facts. She was being kind, and was an obviously experienced nurse. And she was generously giving her free time to assist a patient who was being a pain in the neck — herself.

Now pull yourself together, Jennifer. Nurse Mary doesn't want any more demonstration of your fear — she knows about that and is sympathetic. Or any more excuses as to why you are baulking at the offer they are giving you. No, all she and Mr Sharman want is your decision. So that she can get home to bed for the rest she badly needs.

What shall I do?

Jenny had felt lonely a few days ago — but she wasn't now. So many people seemed to care about her welfare. Wanted to help her when an accident had threatened to make her lame.

A few days ago, she'd overcome her fear to drive so that she could help William, when the boy was helpless, frightened and lost. Now they had come to offer her aid at a time when she felt lost and afraid.

'Come along now, Jenny.' Sister Mary's voice broke into her thoughts. 'Let me take the samples I need. It won't commit you to having the operation. You can decide on that later.'

Jenny sighed as she sat up and looked into Mary's big brown eyes pleading with her to submit to what she'd come to do. The nurse looked very tired and keeping her waiting wasn't fair.

Make up your mind. Make up your mind!

'I . . . I suppose I should,' Jenny said weakly.

'Roll up your sleeve,' Mary said, busy tearing wrappers and placing her wares neatly on the table. 'I have three phials to fill.'

Gritting her teeth, Jenny did as she was told.

'Look out of the window, there's a rainbow in the sky.'

Jenny looked and frowned. 'Really? I can't see one . . . '

Mary chuckled. 'Here, press this wad of cotton wool on your arm. It's just to prevent any blood getting on your clothes.'

Looking down Jenny was astounded to see a trickle of her blood oozing out of a tiny puncture in one of the veins in her arm. Her heart thumped. The procedure was over — and it hadn't hurt!

Packing her medical kit away carefully and efficiently, Mary told her the next step was for her to go to the hospital for an X-ray.

'I'm leaving you this pack of information to read. It contains lots of useful advice and some exercises to do.'

She slapped a heavy-looking envelope on the kitchen table. Jenny looked at it dubiously.

Mary clipped her bag closed saying, 'So I'll book you in at the X-ray department for tomorrow morning at ten.'

Heck! Jenny's throat contracted.

'But I can't drive there! I don't even know where it is.'

Mary walked into the hall carrying her belongings and opened the front door, saying cheerily, 'Get a taxi. Ask for the X-ray department.'

Panic set in again. Jenny clutched the hall table for support.

This was awful. She was being coerced into doing something she didn't want to do!

Yet wasn't it the truth that she had decided to go ahead with the operation?

And the sooner it was over, the better . . .

'Thank you, Mary,' she said weakly to the nurse, who had disappeared, closing the door behind her.

On her own, Jenny felt haunted by her fears once more.

Of course, she could do as she liked. She hadn't signed anything. She could back out of this frightening situation. She had plenty of time to think about what she should do.

But had she?

The constant reminder was the pain that kept shooting through her leg every time she tried to move her injured knee. Resting it didn't help. Anyway, she had to get on with her life — not sit about all day.

By the afternoon Jenny had come to the conclusion that she had no choice but to order a taxi and turn up at the hospital at ten the following morning. Thumbing through the battered old phone book to find the hospital number, she suddenly realised that she didn't even know the name of the private hospital she was supposed to be going to . . .

Ring. Ring. Ring.

Someone at the door was in a mighty hurry.

Painfully she got up and went into the hall to find Alexander standing there.

5

Half pleased, and half angry to see the tall, well-suited man with a smile that faded on seeing her hostile expression, she snapped, 'Mr Sharman — it is customary to wait until you are invited in!'

He swept back the hair that fell over his eyes saying, 'I apologise. I'm just in a bit of a hurry as I have an appointment with William's headmaster to talk about the bullying he suffered on Friday. But first I wanted to tell you that I'm able to take you to the hospital for your X-rays tomorrow morning.'

'Oh, are you now?'

Puzzled, Alexander queried, 'I thought you wanted to go?'

'Look, Mr Sharman, I don't like being bullied!'

There was silence as he frowned down at her. He opened his mouth to say something and then closed it again as though he didn't know what to say to her accusation.

Jenny took a deep breath in.

'You don't seem to understand that I only met you the other day. You asked me to help you out with using my car to find your son — which I did. End of story.'

He gave a lengthy sigh. His deep voice sounded sincere.

'I was grateful for your help, Jenny. I feel I owe you for your kindness. By arranging for you to have a knee operation you very obviously need, I thought I was helping you!'

She swallowed, noticing his embarrassment. Softening her tone, she said, 'Listen. I'm not a member of your family — in fact you are a stranger to me, as I am to you.'

He cleared his throat.

'I don't think you are correct about that. I've got to know you pretty well. And my brother tells me I am not wrong about you needing a new knee.

Now even if you hate my guts, you still have to get to the hospital tomorrow morning and I'll be here at nine-thirty to pick you up, Miss Warner.'

With that statement, he turned around smartly and left her standing open-mouthed.

The heavy phone book slipped out of her hand and dropped onto her toe. Ouch!

He was right — she was wrong. She shouldn't have been so incredibly rude to him. He was trying to reward her for her good turn to him. And she did need a taxi tomorrow morning.

Her misery didn't lift until that evening, watching a film. Then she pulled herself together and ordered some groceries online.

It was difficult for her to get to sleep, knowing she had to rise early to be ready to face a day she wasn't looking forward to.

Should she order a taxi to take her to the hospital in the morning? Had Alexander taken offence at her attitude, her ungrateful demand that she be left to her own devices, and withdrawn his offer? She would just have to see.

* * *

As arranged, Alexander pressed her doorbell at exactly nine-thirty, and waited patiently outside for her to hobble to the door to answer it.

'Good morning, Miss Warner.' He bowed like a Regency gentleman and turned to wait at the top of the steps to help her down.

Jenny was ready to go. She'd been ready for hours, it seemed. Only somehow she still hadn't decided what to say to him.

'I'm sorry about what I said to you yesterday,' she managed to say between the groans at the stabs of pain she felt going downstairs. 'It is very kind of you to fetch me this morning.'

'I understand. You're under stress,' he replied shortly.

She thought he probably was, too.

Maybe it wasn't easy for him to take time off work to take her to hospital. Or — just as likely — he didn't fancy chauffeuring a bad-tempered woman around, on top of having three young children to cope with.

His four-wheeled drive car looked impressive — until Jenny got in. What a mess — and the pong!

He must have noticed her recoil.

'Yes, I know my car is badly in in need of valeting. I'm sorry I haven't had time to do it.'

She thought he needed to tell his children to pick up their debris. Food and sweet wrappers littered the interior of the car. Small, muddy Wellington boots lay in the front passenger footwell. On the back seat were toys and bits of this and that, and a half-eaten sandwich that needed binning. And he'd only just got it back from the garage where it had been serviced! No wonder he thought her car was magnificent.

Still, the mess did take her mind off

worrying about where they were heading.

It wasn't long before Alexander swung into the hospital car park. There was a space reserved for Mr Sharman — his brother — but Alexander parked in it.

Reception were expecting her and she was whisked away for her X-rays with a very charming radiographer, who gently completed what she had to do without giving her any pain at all.

'That's it. Now I'll show you the way back to reception.'

Back in the spacious, lounge-like reception area, Jenny felt unexpectedly miffed to see so many of the staff making a fuss of Alexander. Half a dozen women were laughing and chatting to him while he enjoyed a large frothy coffee and a biscuit.

'Would you like a coffee?' Jenny was asked. She shook her head, although she would have liked one. She knew she mustn't keep Alexander waiting as he had to get back to work.

'OK?' he asked, getting up with a look of genuine concern on his face.

As the staff melted away, Jenny said contritely, 'I apologise for my snappiness this morning. Thank you for waiting but I can get a taxi home, honestly.'

He grinned. Then he bent over and gave her a light kiss on her cheek, which made her blush.

'Forget it. I want to take you home — it's on the way to my next appointment anyway.'

So once again Jenny was ushered into his disgracefully dirty car. She presumed he was so used to it, he didn't think it was repulsive.

She looked sideways at him as he concentrated on driving. He was good-looking and had an easy charm, as she'd noticed the hospital staff appreciating. But he also looked tired, and she was reminded that he had recently lost his wife.

He had the burden of looking after three young children who were clearly running circles around him. Perhaps he was afraid they might not like being told to behave, and so he felt he had to spoil them. However, just like puppies and kittens, they needed training. She smiled at him.

'Thank you, Alexander, for giving up your time to take me to hospital this morning. I will endeavour to have the operation your brother has kindly arranged for me — without making any more fuss. I can get up the stairs on my own, though, so please don't wait.'

He parked outside the house and rushed around to help her get out.

'It's no bother — '

'Alexander. I am quite capable of walking up the stairs. And I don't like you treating me like someone I have to obey. Let's get this straight — I can manage.'

He laughed.

'Right. And let's get this straight. I am at your service, madam, should you ever need me.'

He didn't give her time to comment

as he slid back into his car and reversed neatly. Waving cheerfully, he was gone.

She stood leaning on the wall, wishing he had escorted her up to her flat. Being proud and independent was all very well, and memories of her controlling ex were still vivid — but everyone needed help at times.

Jenny thought Alexander probably did need help with his life, just as she had found she needed it.

She resolved to be a good patient and do all she was told to do, so that she recovered from her operation as quickly as possible. Then she might find that she could assist him in some way. It gave her a goal.

As her operation was to be soon, she busied herself preparing for it. One piece of information in the packet she had been given was about a nursing home where she could go straight afterwards to recuperate. It would be a bit like staying at a hotel, as she would have no work to do, her meals would be prepared for her, and nurses around to help her if necessary as she became used to her new knee.

Jenny wasn't sure exactly where in the world her father was, but she sent him a message to say that she was going into hospital. So as not to worry him unduly, she added that it was for straightforward knee surgery. She received a reply immediately, sending her his love and wishing her all the best. He hoped to return to England to see her before long, and he was thinking about retiring sometime in the near future — the usual vague promises she'd heard so many times.

Leaving her flat for a while required preparation, just as if she was going on a long holiday. Ironically she hadn't taken a holiday since winning her fortune. She hadn't felt like one — although she always had it in the back of her mind to do some travelling.

To tell the truth, she didn't fancy going anywhere on her own. She would meet other travellers, of course; some holidays were designed especially for single people like herself. But what she really longed for was a true friend to accompany her, and she hadn't met anyone yet who fulfilled that need.

Debating whether she should hobble downstairs to chat to Mrs Sharman, whom she was sure would already know about her impending temporary absence, she decided to write her a short letter and enclosed a cheque for her rent in advance. That way she didn't have to discuss her relationship with both of her sons.

She liked her landlady and didn't want to upset her. What her sons may have said about her, she didn't like to contemplate!

Busy planning for leaving her flat, filling a suitcase with essential clothes and making sure the fridge was emptied of anything that didn't keep, occupied Jenny until tea time when she suddenly realised Alexander would be arriving shortly to pick William up after school.

Sitting to the side of the front bay window, she found she could see part of the front of the house, and the drive. Although she'd had a cup of tea, and would have liked another, she preferred to remain looking out for him rather than leaving her observation post and possibly missing seeing him.

A couple of hours went by. By turns she massaged her knee and rested her elbows on the windowsill.

It's my own fault that I'm behaving like a lovesick teenager. I shouldn't have attacked him in the way I did.

Now he knows what a temper I have, can I blame him from steering clear of me?

I made it clear that he was not to interfere in my life. I have got my wish as he is obviously staying away from me.

The sharp ring on her mobile made her start.

'Hello,' she said eagerly.

But it was a secretary from the hospital informing her that an ambulance would be coming to take her to the private hospital early next morning.

★ ★ ★

Anxiety kept Jenny awake until the early hours. She felt almost glad when it was time for her to get up and prepare to leave. Having something positive to do was preferable to lying awake and feeling guilty about her poor attitude to dealing with her bad luck of injuring her knee — and the people who were trying to help her.

With the determination to face the unpleasantness of the operation and co-operate fully with the medics, Jenny went off to hospital a changed woman. She felt she'd grown in stature. Her future looked promising, once the ordeal was over and her leg was better.

In a private room at the hospital, she was told by the cheerful nurses what they wanted her to do before she went to theatre. It was a long wait, but they put the television on for her.

When there was a knock on the door and Mr James Sharman walked in, Jenny felt cowed. His professional charm and willingness to reassure her before she signed the documents to allow him to operate made her confident that he would do a skilled job.

He didn't stay long, and when he'd gone she felt honoured that he had fitted her in on his list, as she'd been told he had.

How could she have mistaken Mr Sharman's efficiency for arrogance, and missed his kindness when she'd first met him?

6

Several days later, Jenny was recovering in the nursing home, enjoying the high standard of care and feeling optimistic that her new knee was going to be fine.

But the better she felt physically, the more she began to consider her future. It might not be necessary for her to leave her flat after all. After the physiotherapists had shown her the exercises she had to do, and got her up walking around, she realised she would be able to climb stairs just as she used to before she injured her knee. Fantastic!

'There's ever such a handsome man and a young boy in Reception, wanting to know if you'd like to see them,' said a nurse putting her head around Jenny's private room door.

Not having had many visitors, as she had no family to come and see her and just a couple of friends who'd been kind enough to make the long journey from town, Jenny wondered if the nurse had made a mistake.

'I'll bring them up to your room, or you can go downstairs to the lounge if you like — '

'I'll go down. Will you pass me my crutches?'

As the nurse helped her walk to the lift and assisted her into the lounge, Jenny suddenly wished she'd thought to make herself look more presentable. She was dressed, but in casual clothes. She should have combed her hair and put a smear of lipstick on.

Too late now to worry about her appearance. Her mind switched to wondering who her visitors could be.

The first thing she saw was a boy dressed in school uniform, seeing what he could get out of the snack machine, with his dad keeping an eye on him while clutching a bouquet of flowers.

Her heart pounded. It couldn't be the Sharmans — could it?

William, who noticed her first, cried, 'There she is, Dad!'

Alexander's smile almost made her cry. It was so many things: alight with pleasure at seeing her, hesitant in case she was cross that he'd come . . . and sexy! If she hadn't fancied him before, she certainly did now.

He crossed the room in a few strides and assisted her to sit on one of the sofas. William bounced down beside her and taking out a crumpled envelope, he handed it to her saying, 'I made you a get-well card in the art class when the teacher wasn't looking.'

'Oh! Thank you, William,' she said, genuinely touched that he'd thought of her. Although his card would win no art prizes, the words he'd written couldn't have been sweeter:

To Miss Warner,

We hope your new knee is fabulous and you will come and visit us soon.

Love from William, and Kate and Toby (my brother and sister).

'It's lovely, William — thank you.'

Jenny wanted to give his red cheek a kiss but knew a twelve-year-old would not appreciate one and said so.

'You can kiss me, if you like,' said Alexander cheerfully, as he handed her the bouquet.

To her amazement Jenny found no difficulty in complying as she leaned over, the flowers in her hand, and placed her lips on his cheek. Then she blushed, as she said, 'Thank you.'

William said unceremoniously, 'Now we've seen Miss Warner, can we go home, Dad? May I have your car keys?'

Alexander shook his head and laughed.

'No, William. I would like to talk to Miss Warner for a few more minutes. Go and ask at reception for a vase for Miss Warner's flowers which can be taken up to her room.'

When William had left them, he turned to look deeply into her eyes. 'William is keen to drive on the road, but he'll have to wait for five years before he has driving lessons.'

Jenny remarked, 'He's a bright lad.'

Alexander beamed with pride. 'Yes, he is. He won a scholarship to the school he is attending, that's why I still take him into London every day. Polly — his mum — and I thought he should be given the opportunity to have an academic education to the fullest of his ability. And I continue to take him to his school as he is a pain in the neck for his grandparents, who look after Kate and Toby after school until I get home in the evening.'

Jenny began to piece together his family. Polly was his former wife, William, Kate and Toby their children. Polly's parents, the children's grandparents, were helping Alexander out by babysitting for him — and by the sounds of it, they couldn't manage William. Oh dear!

'May I repeat William's request that you visit us when you are able to drive?'

Jenny answered, 'Thank you.' But in her mind, she put the brakes on. Was this an attempt for her to be persuaded to become a nursemaid for his children? Because she didn't want that! She had got away from Marvin and his manipulative nature, and there was no way she wanted to find her neck in another noose.

He'd gone behind her back to arrange for his brother to operate on her leg. He'd made sure she would be well cared for in this well-run nursing home after the operation. Oh yes, indeed, she appreciated how he'd made sure she was taken care of, even taking time off work and all the while having to cope with his family commitments — which was good of him.

It showed he was kind-hearted. Too kind-hearted, perhaps? Was overlooking his children's behaviour the right thing to do, even though they would be missing their mother? Jenny had lost her mother when she was a teenager and knew how much it hurt.

However, she wondered, didn't anyone have sympathy for Alexander, who had the burden of coping with his grief and carrying on running his family as well as his job? And by the sound of it, Polly's parents were being helpful — up to a point. They found William a handful and would only deal with the younger children.

So Alexander needed someone to straighten his kids out. He had to find the right kind of person — or perhaps he could send them to boarding school, which would make a different kind of life for them all. But what if Polly had asked him not to do that?

Jenny felt she ought to agree to visit his home, meet all his family, and then she would know the situation and whether she could be of any help to them. It would certainly give her a better picture of the man she knew in her heart she had become infatuated with. Because that was a decision she would have to face: learn to accept him as he was, with his family, or lose him.

'Certainly I'd like to visit you,' she said.

He smiled. 'I'll let you know when

Jim says it is right for you to drive, and how to get to us.'

There he was again, arranging things for her! She bristled, then made herself stop and think. He was trying to help her — not make all the decisions in her life, as Marvin had tried to do.

She sighed, knowing it was up to her to decide what she wanted. First of all, she had to find out more about Alexander before she would know if she wanted to live with him. And he, too, would need to decide what he wanted.

Jenny looked into his eyes.

'What job do you do? You seem to be able to take time off when you want to.'

'I'm a surveyor. I have to look at buildings and any land adjoining to assess what state it is in before the property is sold. I'm given work to do, but usually have some leeway as to when I actually do it. And write the reports. But, of course, my employers have been very good since Polly died, giving me extra time off when I've asked for it.'

'Mmm. Well, don't use any more of your precious time on me, Alexander. You've been very generous. But now I must stand on my own feet.'

'Of course you must, Jenny! But you still need a little more time to recover after your op. My mother seems to agree that the stairs in her house to your flat will not suit you any more, and you'd be better off in a downstairs flat or a bungalow. But don't think she wants to get rid of you. She'll be very sorry to see you leave.'

Jenny smiled ruefully.

'As I will, leaving her house. I can understand she'll be worried about a new tenant.'

William came running back to them.

'Dad, we've got to go to the supermarket — there's nothing in the fridge and I'm hungry.'

Alexander rose and offered Jenny his arm as she took her crutches, saying, 'William is right. I can't let my family starve — and they get through an enormous number of ready meals. I have to go shopping more than once a week.'

Jenny was about to protest that ready meals were unnecessarily expensive — but who was at home to cook his family a nourishing meal?

She felt a pang of loss as they departed. She placed William's crumpled Get Well card on her bedside table near the vase of flowers.

'Ahh!' she breathed. 'That was kind of them.'

* * *

It was several weeks before Jenny went back to her flat. She'd become so used to the hotel-like service at the nursing home that it was quite a shock for her to find she had to start doing everything for herself once again.

Mrs Sharman welcomed her warmly — and so did the cat.

Mrs Sharman said, 'I got my cleaning lady to get you some bread and milk, which she's put in your fridge. Let me know what else you need. But I expect you'll do some online shopping for groceries, as you usually did.'

Jenny detected a note of reserve in her voice. Probably both her sons had been telling her about her tenant's vulnerability. But she didn't like to admit they had spoken to her.

Mrs Sharman was also rather stressed at the idea that Jenny would be moving. Not for one moment had she thought that young Miss Jenny Warner, whom she liked and got on well with, would have to move out so soon after moving in.

But that first day back in her flat after arriving from the nursing home wasn't a good time for a heart-to-heart. So Jenny just stroked the cat, and thanked the ambulance man who willingly took her bags up to her flat.

'I'll come down and have a chat with you tomorrow, Mrs Sharman,' Jenny said, giving her a smile. 'I'm pleased to be back here,' she added, as the ambulance man offered her his arm to make sure she climbed the stairs with him safely.

Once alone in her apartment, Jenny breathed contentedly. But she was tired after the move and only pottered about for a short while before retiring for a good night's rest.

* * *

In the morning Jenny's mind was clearer.

Alexander came into her mind first. She went to her front window to see if his car was there, then remembered. *Of course, he won't be coming until he picks up William after school. How silly of me!*

She had lots to do to get her flat back as it was before she went into hospital, so she didn't think of him again until after lunch.

Anxiously going over to the window to look down at the drive, Jenny remembered she'd told Mrs Sharman that she'd go down to have a chat with her. She wished she'd thought of it earlier. It would be embarrassing to go down now and find William there and Alexander due any moment. The last thing she wanted was to seem as though she was chasing him.

Well, she hadn't mentioned a time when she would go to see Mrs Sharman, so maybe it would be best to wait until the early evening, when Alexander and his son had left.

It was going to be a bit like walking a tightrope, not showing too much interest in him but also to let him feel she was keen to develop their relationship — yet she was dying to see him!

She jumped at the sharp ring of the doorbell.

Surely it couldn't be . . .

But when she cautiously opened the door, there he stood — like a salesman, well back from the door.

His vivid blue eyes fixed on hers, Alexander said, 'I hope you had a good night and that your knee is not bothering you.'

'Hello — er, no it's not.' She had difficulty tearing her gaze from his. She noted he'd had a haircut, and the thick locks were now neatly in place. Nevertheless he still brushed back the hair on his forehead — out of habit, she guessed. Perhaps, like her, he felt awkward not knowing how their relationship was going to pan out.

Jenny swallowed. 'Is your family well?'

He grinned. 'Chaotic. As usual.'

'Don't you have anyone to help you?'

He nodded. 'Yes, we have a daily help — Rosie. And Polly's parents, Joan and Cyril.'

'So you don't need me,' Jenny said and immediately blushed scarlet. Whatever had made her say that?

'Oh, I wouldn't say that!' He laughed and gave her a saucy wink.

To delay any further decision about her visit, Jenny said, 'I have to recover and feel confident about using my car.'

'I could fetch you.'

'No, Alexander you've already given a

lot of your time to help me — and I'm most grateful. But I must practise driving short distances in my sports car until I am able to spread my wings. Then I'll pop over and see you and the kids.'

He sighed. 'Well if that's the way you want it.'

'I do.' She felt she had to make it clear that she was independent, well able to make her own decisions. He must accept her refusal to be manipulated by him.

Then, noticing a shadow passing over his face, she felt immediately contrite. No way did she want him to think she was trying to avoid meeting his family — nor that she wasn't keen to be friends with him. She might be in love with him, but it was a romance that had only just begun. And it may be doomed when she met his family!

He moved as if to leave, then swung around and said humbly, 'May I visit you here?'

'Well, as long as I am here. I'm

looking for a new apartment on the ground floor.'

'I can help you with that, Jenny.'

Of course he could. Wasn't he a surveyor?

From downstairs William yelled, 'I hope your knee is better, Miss Warner. Granny won't let me come up to see you.'

Jenny yelled back. 'Thanks, William.'

'Must go.' Alexander gave a quick wave and trotted down the stairs.

Guilt struck Jenny when he'd disappeared. Had she dismissed him too callously when he was clearly trying to encourage her to meet his family?

Sighing, she determined to get hold of the driving school and book a few refresher lessons as soon as she had the surgeon's nod.

Looking out of the window, she saw Alexander's car leaving and sighed again.

A little later she went down and knocked on Mrs Sharman's door.

'My dear, I didn't expect to see you

so soon. Do come in.'

Jenny was glad to sit down in her kitchen and watch Mrs Sharman finish her ironing.

'So, Miss Warner, how was the operation? Not too bad for you, I hope?'

Jenny laughed. 'Please call me Jenny, Mrs Shaman. I feel part of your family now.'

Mrs Sharman plonked down the iron and, turning to her, smiled. 'I hoped you would say that. They are all very fond of you.'

'Well, I have to thank your surgeon son. He did a brilliant job on my knee. Look.'

Jenny pulled up her skirt to reveal her slender leg and the scar running over the knee. 'When he visited me in the nursing home, he said the scar would almost disappear in time.'

Mrs Sharman folded the garment she'd been ironing and put it on the pile of freshly pressed clothes, then took another crumpled shirt from the basket, gave it a shake and began ironing it.

'Mrs Sharman. I expect you know, Alexander and William have asked me to go and visit them — soon.'

'Yes, I know they asked you.'

Jenny said outright what was uppermost in her mind.

'I don't want to be nosy, but I would like to know if you think it is right for him to introduce me to his in-laws so soon after losing his wife?'

Mrs Sharman stopped ironing and gazed into space. Then she said, 'I am a widow and know how difficult it is when the person you lived with and loved has died. So I can only tell you from my own experience and feelings about the situation . . . ' She looked out of the kitchen window at the racing clouds. 'My opinion is that I would have been happy if Polly had not died. She was a lovely girl and a good mother. Always nice to me, and my husband when he was alive.' She gave a sigh then continued, 'But tragedies happen. Polly was taken from us, and now Alexander has to re plan his life. Not easy for him with three children.'

'No, it is not,' Jenny agreed emphatically.

His mother gave another sigh and continued, 'I expect he has not ruled out remarrying. And when the right woman for him comes along, he may well ask her.'

Jenny looked down at her hands and squeezed her fingers. 'How soon would be . . . correct for him to be looking again?'

Mrs Sharman gave a chuckle. 'No rules about that, my dear. Could be years — or maybe he has already chosen the woman he wants.'

Feeling she was almost tumbling into her thoughts, Jenny said quickly, 'You don't think I'd be pushing into his life too soon by going to visit him and his family in the next couple of weeks?'

Resuming her ironing, Mrs Sharman said, 'Not if you want to. Everyone has to make up their own minds about such things.' After a pause, she added, 'You are a sensible young lady, Jenny. Whatever you do will be right for you . . . however long it takes.'

That was putting the ball squarely back into her court, Jenny realised. At least she knew Mrs Sharman was not opposed to her involving herself with her son's family.

⋆   ⋆   ⋆

At last the day arrived when Jenny began to drive with more confidence. First she made short trips to the supermarket, then she ventured further afield and felt quite proud of herself as she scooted around. She never really liked her sports car, it was far too showy, but at least after her extra lessons she could manoeuvre and park it anywhere with ease, get it filled up with petrol, and understand all the dashboard indicators.

Alexander didn't pester her — in fact he seemed to be keeping a low profile, just as she'd asked. Now she had to inform him that she was ready to travel to his house in the village of Thrompton, in the western commuter belt of London.

She felt quite excited about the trip, thinking over and over again what she should wear and what gifts she should bring — because children always expected a gift, however small. She thought long and hard, and decided a present for them all to treasure was called for.

She mentioned it quite casually to Mrs Sharman that she hoped Alexander would ask her to visit now that she felt roadworthy.

Coming home late one afternoon, she found a note shoved into her letterbox.

Delighted to welcome you this weekend — stay as long as you like. Enclosed is a map showing how to get to us.

Love, Alexander, William, Kate and Toby

Jenny trembled as she read it. She had invited herself — but he had snapped up the offer.

He had another thought coming if he had in mind for her to stay more than a few hours. For one thing, she had to drive home in the evening and she knew that Saturday evening going back into London, driving solo, would be a test of courage for her.

She would wear her comfortable jeans, a shirt and a leather jacket that would look smart yet casual. She would take a change of shoes and a cardigan in a small bag. Then whatever the weather or whatever the family did, such as going for a walk after lunch, she would manage.

She looked forward to a relaxing weekend.

7

On Saturday morning Jenny suddenly had a brainwave. If she was going to Thrompton maybe she could take the family's cat, Belle, along. The children would love to have Polly's pet back with them, and it would save Mrs Sharman the worry of looking after a restless cat for a while.

Mrs Sharman thought it was a splendid idea and found Belle's cat carrier in the garage, aired it and washed the cat's blanket. Belle wasn't so sure about the move — but then Belle didn't know she was going home, did she?

Packed in her car with a holdall and the gifts, Jenny drove off with Mrs Sharman at the door waving her goodbye.

Soon away from the busy traffic, she began to feel more relaxed. The weather was autumnal, and there was a freshness in the air as Jenny drove out into the countryside. Red, yellow and russet-coloured leaves were flying off the trees and forming mounds at the sides of the roads.

Thrompton was just outside a fair-sized town and not signposted until she'd almost got there. The cat had been complaining all the journey. Suddenly she realised she hadn't any cat food and maybe the family hadn't any either, so she stopped at a supermarket to get some. And some sweets for the kids.

Seeing the green fields dotted with sheep and harvesting work going on in the countryside fascinated her — not that she felt she wanted to give up her town life, which she was used to.

Finally, in the centre of the village she asked for directions to Wayside Cottage. Some children playing football on the green pointed out the narrow lane.

Alexander's country house took her

breath away. Nestled between farm-land and tall trees, it was a house made by knocking together three cottages. Standing solid as Victorian buildings do, it had modern additions like a double garage and a wide drive in front of the house.

'You're home, Belle.' Jenny told the cat, which blinked at her as if recognising the country smells.

Her legs felt a bit shaky as she got out of the car and stood breathing in the clear country air. No one came out to greet her so she went to the front door, admiring the climbing mauve wisteria curtaining the porch, and rang the bell.

Where was everyone? Had she made a mistake about the day she was due to come? Perhaps they were out and didn't expect her until later?

Having come all this way, Jenny didn't feel like going back to London. She had been invited here so she gently opened the door, listening for sounds of a radio or TV. But the place was silent.

'Hello,' she called out. 'Anyone at home?'

Maybe they had gone shopping and would return any moment. She crept in, thinking it gave her the chance to have a quick look at Alexander's family home.

There were signs that the occupants were not tidy people. She almost tripped over a toy fire engine left on the floor.

Making her way along a corridor, she came to an open door leading into a huge kitchen with windows onto the garden at the far end. A beautiful family room — or it should have been, except for the mess everywhere!

She wouldn't have worn her new cream wool jacket if she'd known that every surface was dirty and liable to mark it.

'My goodness!' she said out loud.

Suddenly she felt cross. Had Alexander deliberately left his house messy so that she should see he needed her help?

Looking out of the kitchen patio window, her attention was captured by the sight of a small boy running towards her. He must be Toby.

He didn't notice her until he arrived panting on the kitchen patio. His little face registered surprise and then he seemed to remember a guest was due.

He looked up into her face, saying, 'Good morning, Miss Warner,' as if he'd been schooled to greet her. Then he added, 'What time is it? Dad wants to know.'

Jenny looked at her watch.

'Half past twelve. Where is your father?'

Toby pointed outside.

'We're having a bonfire. A big bonfire with flames. We've got lots of garden stuff to burn. Katie likes to dance around it.'

Jenny could imagine the fun it must be for the kids.

Without more ado, Toby darted off.

I suppose if I want a cup of coffee I'd better make one, Jenny thought and looked around for the kettle and coffee and milk. It struck her that the kitchen had been well laid out — it was just neglected, which she supposed was only to be expected after Polly had died. No one was using her cooking things.

Clearing a space on the kitchen table to put her mug down, she sat and sipped her drink — but not for long, as she spied Alexander racing towards the house, followed by a little girl and Toby.

'Gosh! I'm so sorry I wasn't here to greet you,' she heard Alexander say as he gasped for breath. 'I lost track of the time.' Removing his Wellington boots, he stepped into the kitchen and stooped to kiss her cheek. 'Nice to see you, Jenny.'

Then he started to look around the kitchen, noticing the remains of cooked breakfasts on the plates that hadn't been put in the dishwasher.

'Drat the boy!' he muttered. Then turning to Jenny, he said, 'Come into the sitting room. We were anxious to start the bonfire and haven't cleared up after breakfast. William promised me he would do it — but you know what boys are!'

Seeing his embarrassment at the state of the kitchen, Jenny didn't like to say that boys may get away with disobeying their parents at times, but she had the strong suspicion that young William needed taking in hand. But she was glad to see Alexander, even with his hair tousled, his old jersey ragged and his jeans with splits at the knees. Appearances didn't matter; her heart was telling her to look under the untidiness. And what she saw was a decent young man, caring about his family and doing his best after losing his beloved wife.

'Take your coffee with you and sit down. Toby and Katie, you go and wash your hands and then talk to Miss Warner while William and I prepare the lunch.'

The two younger children scampered off and Alexander escorted Jenny into their sitting room — a charming, low-beamed room with a large open fireplace and easy leather and chinz-covered chairs.

'Take your pick,' Alexander said, whipping some toys off the sofa, as she chose to sit there.

Katie came rushing in.

'I want to sit by Miss Warner,' she announced.

'So do I,' said Toby who'd followed her in.

Sitting with an eager child either side of her was a new experience for Jenny, but she found to her delight that they were chatty and funny.

'Dad, I want the fish and chips,' Katie called to her father.

'So do I,' Toby said.

Alexander stood by the door and explained. 'We went out to the super-market early this morning and got some ready meals. A variety so you could have a choice, Jenny. We have some meat pies, beef and chicken, pasta, and fish and chips. Which would you like?'

Aghast, Jenny knew she didn't fancy

any. But she knew in a flash that the expensive meals were a treat for the children and she didn't want to show she was ungrateful for their effort to please her. So she laughed.

'Give me one the children don't like,' she said.

Alexander said with a wink at her, 'I'll treat you to a first class restaurant meal as soon as I can.'

That sounded like a good proposition and Jenny smiled back at him.

It wasn't long before William appeared, his face clean and his red hair plastered down tidily.

'Lunch is served,' he announced.

The family meal in the dining side of the kitchen was fun because the children, however untidy they had become, were a friendly bunch. They had good table manners and tucked into their meals with relish, which was good to see.

'It's nice you've come,' remarked William as he put his knife and fork down on his empty plate. 'I hope your knee is all better now.'

'How kind of you, William. Yes, my leg is almost back to normal, thank you.'

Alexander grinned at her, satisfied that William could behave like a gentleman when he chose to.

'Now, I expect you are ready for the gifts I've brought you,' Jenny said, hoping they wouldn't notice she hadn't eaten more than a mouthful or two of the mutton pie. She was used to cooking her own meals with fresh meat and vegetables. Simple but tasty dishes.

'Presents! Oh, yes, please!'

'Go in the sitting room and I'll light the fire,' Alexander said, getting up and swilling the last of his can of beer.

'What about clearing the meal away?' asked Jenny, starting to collect the plates. She might as well show them from the start that everyone had to help. And they did — although the children were dying to know what she'd brought for them.

118

* * *

A little later, ensconced in the cosy sitting room, the children's eyes sparkled as she gave each their present. No way did she want them to know she was a millionaire, to flash her money around. But after careful thought she decided an enduring personal present and a packet of sweets would be correct, seeing as they had lost their mum recently and deserved a treat.

William was delighted with his smartphone. He'd lost his when the bigger boys had bullied him and thrown his phone in a garden pond. Jenny thought Alexander may have replaced it with a cheap one — but this one she gave him was new on the market. She knew he was a bright lad and would have no trouble learning to use it. With shining eyes, William came up to her full of emotion to mutter, 'Thank you, Miss Warner.'

While Toby showed more appreciation for his carton of sweets, he nevertheless clung to the large box containing an electric train set. Some grown-ups kept their childhood model railways to enjoy as a hobby. Jenny thought young Toby might too.

Katie's delight was obvious at her gold necklace. Although unaware of its value, she assured Jenny that she would treasure it. Jenny explained that as Katie grew older, more links could be added to make the necklace longer.

Alexander, who was well aware of her wealth, didn't seem too overwhelmed to receive an expensive watch. Jenny had noticed his boy-like watch with a worn strap that he would need to replace sooner or later. But this watch had status. An accessory a business man would appreciate.

As they all admired each other's gifts Jenny said quite casually, 'Actually I have another surprise for you all — in my car.'

'More chocolate?' asked Toby eagerly.

Jenny was about to rise, when William said, 'Shall I get it from your car, Miss Warner?'

'Well, it's pretty heavy, and you must bring it in very carefully, and not knock it.'

'Oh, I will. May I have your car keys, please?'

'I left them in the ignition.'

As William darted out, followed by the other two children, Alexander came and sat by her on the sofa.

'It is very kind of you, Jenny, to give us all such expensive presents — and don't say you can afford it. The point is, they were chosen with care and we really appreciate your generosity.'

'Don't tell the children I'm well off.'

He shook his head.

'I haven't and I won't. The last thing I want is for you to think your wealth is desirable for me. I earn a good salary and have no need to beg, borrow or steal anything from you!'

Looking deeply into each other's eyes for a moment or two it seemed as if a pact was being made between them.

Suddenly Jenny asked, 'Do you like

the watch? You can change it for another model if you prefer.'

'It's magnificent!'

He proceeded to demonstrate why the watch was so special and he was proud to own it.

Squeals from outside made him rush to look out of the window.

'What on earth . . . ' He began to look worried.

Katie came tearing in, her eyes sparkling

'Dad . . . Miss Warner has brought our cat home!'

'I hope you don't mind, Alexander. Your mum seemed quite pleased to hand Belle over to you for a few days.'

He didn't get a chance to reply. The cat yowled as she was gently taken out of her cat carrier and the small hands that stroked her eagerly showed how thrilled the children were to have her back with them. Belle, too, seemed happy to be back in her home, and Jenny felt she should not be moved again. Surely they could look after her?

Teach the children to feed her, and put a cat flap in the kitchen door so she could go out hunting when she wanted to?

'I don't know if there is any cat food,' said Alexander ruefully.

'Don't worry. I brought some with me. But Belle will require a dish of water right now, as I expect she is thirsty after her ride over here.'

Katie said, 'My mum always used put her food over by the patio door in the corner where she would be undisturbed. There is her cat flap, so she can go out in the garden when she wants.'

Belle was glad of a drink and purred loudly then she took a stroll around her home, looking around for her basket. And, Jenny realised, for Polly. It almost made her cry to see the little animal missing her mistress who wasn't there to greet her.

She also noticed the tears in Alexander's eyes as he turned away with a handkerchief up to his face as he said croakily, 'I'll go and find Belle's basket.

I think I put it in the garage.'

William said gleefully, 'I'll get Belle's cat food from your car, Miss Warner.' Off he sped and Jenny was pleased he was removed from the scene of his father's show of emotion. The two younger children seemed unaware of it as they cuddled Belle, now purring loudly.

When Alexander came in with the cat basket everyone returned to the fireside in the sitting room. They had only just settled when there was a tremendous crash from outside.

'What on earth was that?'

A scream could be heard as Alexander leapt up and dived to look out of the front window.

'Oh my God!'

Jenny and the children rushed to the window to try and see what had happened. Alexander had fled out of the room towards the front door.

Jenny restrained Katie and Toby from running after him.

'Stay here,' she ordered, and to her

surprise they obeyed her.

She wanted to go out, but had the feeling there had been an accident outside the cottage and she didn't want the little ones to be involved.

'You look after Belle,' she said, making all three, Toby, Katie and the cat, sit on the hearth rug by the fire. 'Make sure she doesn't escape while your father deals with whatever is going on out there.'

Once again Jenny was relieved the two young children didn't argue. Two pairs of eyes looked at her as if she had the right to tell them what to do. As she hurried outside as best she could with her tender knee, she called back at them in a calm voice, 'Look after Belle. Make sure she stays in here with you.'

Still hearing no protest from the children, Jenny closed the sitting room door firmly as she made her way through the hall towards the front door, her heart pounding as she heard another scream.

Raised voices warned her she was

about to get a shock. Stepping out into the drive, she noticed her car wasn't where she'd parked it.

'Agh!'

No wonder, because it had moved forward with some force and was now on end as it had collided with a tree!

Images jumped into her mind of what must have happened. Young William had been playing about with the car keys and had started the engine. Being automatic — which he probably hadn't realised — the car had leapt forward and smashed into the tree!

Seeing Alexander bending over the driver's door made her aware that William had probably been hurt. The boy's cries confirmed her suspicion.

The back of the car looked normal enough — but the front was crumpled against the big oak tree. She saw Alexander straighten up and take the mobile from his pocket.

Jenny walked nearer. Then she saw the blood on Alexander's shirt front and quailed.

Get a grip, she told herself sternly.

Her recent experience in hospital had taught her a great deal about medical matters she'd previously dreaded. She steeled herself to cope with whatever she saw.

Remain calm, she instructed herself. *Assist Alexander, who must be terribly worried about his son — quite apart from his anger at him.*

Crunching over the gravel towards her car, it became apparent that it was a write-off — the engine shattered.

Going to the passenger side, she could see William's head lolling over the steering wheel. His cries had ceased, replaced by quieter moans of pain, and sobs of, 'I'm sorry!'

'I've phoned for the ambulance and they'll be here as soon as they can.' Alexander snapped his mobile shut and put it in his jeans pocket.

His tortured eyes found Jenny's and he added, 'They say not to move him, just reassure him and keep him as comfortable as possible.'

Squatting down, he spoke gently to the boy.

Jenny couldn't hear what was said, but she realised her presence wasn't needed.

'I'll go back and keep an eye on Katie and Toby — make sure they don't come out here.'

'Good idea.' Alexander shot her a grateful smile.

Having the presence of mind to open the car boot — with difficulty, as the catch was way in the air — Jenny managed to haul out the box of cat food and walked back into the house.

Whatever injuries William had suffered, Alexander was with him to comfort him and wait for the ambulance to arrive — which may take a while in this rural area.

Her job was to look after Katie and Toby — and the cat too. It was daunting. She knew nothing about childcare. Nor cats, for that matter.

The smaller children were dying to know what had happened, and Jenny was careful not to criticise William as she explained. Their brother had driven her car into the big tree outside.

'Why?'

Jenny tried not to sound too dramatic.

'I guess when he went to get the cat food he thought he might start the engine for fun. But he shouldn't have, as the car jumped forward and smashed into the tree trunk.'

'Is William going to die?'

As the children had just lost their mother, the last thing she wanted was to scare them. She smiled reassuringly at the looks of horror on their little faces. 'Oh no! He's just been injured.'

Katie wanted to know if William was badly hurt.

Toby said, 'I want to see him.'

'No, you can't go outside,' Jenny said firmly when they begged her to let them go.

'Why can't we?'

'Your dad told me to tell you to stay here.'

'Why?'

Jenny sighed. 'Because the ambulance is due soon and the paramedics won't want anyone in their way.'

'What's a paramedic?' asked Katie.

'A kind of travelling doctor, or nurse, who take an ambulance to accidents and help any injured people.'

'Will he have crutches like you, Miss Warner?'

'We'll have to wait and see. Now let's go and get you some supper, and feed Belle.'

'There are no more ready meals,' said Katie.

'How about me cooking you something?'

Both children looked interested.

'Wow! Can you cook, Miss Warner?'

She nodded. 'Some things.'

'Like what?' Katie asked.

'I'm not eating porridge!' cried Toby. 'No way. That's what Granny makes us for breakfast and it's horrible.'

Jenny chuckled. 'Let me suggest some things you may like. What about cheese toasties, or scrambled egg . . . '

Belatedly she wondered what Alexander had in his fridge or store cupboard. A quick search determined that it was very little!

She said brightly, 'I can make you some pancakes. They are nice . . . '

8

Cooking with her mind on two scenes, one outside the house with Alexander and his injured son, and the other with Alexander's two other children, Jenny struggled to get the supper.

If it wasn't for Katie being a bossy little madam, and Toby a good-natured little boy, Jenny might have found the task more difficult.

'I know where Mum kept most things,' Katie told Jenny, as she proceeded to open each of the kitchen cupboards to show Jenny what was in them. Meanwhile Toby was happy feeding the cat.

Pancakes provided added entertainment as the children wanted to toss them in the air.

They were soon eating pancakes that tasted perfectly all right, although they wouldn't have won a cookery contest.

When a siren sounded outside, Jenny had to grab hold of Katie's arm as she scampered to the kitchen door.

'Wait! Your father will be in shortly, and he will tell you how William is.'

The only way Jenny could take their minds off bolting outside was to order them — quite severely — to help her clean up the kitchen. Fortunately, they had a dishwasher — but they had to help empty all the clean lunch dishes out of it first.

Jenny heard Alexander stomp into the house. He went into the sitting room first, then realising they were in the kitchen he barged in, anxiety written all over his face.

Jenny's heart went out to him. She would have hugged him, only they were not on those terms. She could only meet his worry-filled eyes and try to show her sympathy.

As all eyes were on him he cleared his throat and announced, 'William has to go to hospital to have his arm seen to.'

'Dad,' piped up Katie. 'Will he die?'

Toby's eyes were as round as plates.

A smile emerged on Alexander's features.

'Heavens, no! He's been injured, and your Uncle Jim is going to see him and make sure his arm is fixed.' He swung around and said to Jenny, 'Unlike your car — which I'm sorry to say is a write-off.'

He pushed his fingers through his hair and muttered something about having to get her a replacement, but Jenny said clearly, 'You know I never liked that car. It will give me the excuse to buy one I do like, won't it?'

'Get another red one — I like red,' Katie said.

Jenny had already poured Alexander a cup of tea and, going up to him, said, 'Drink this — it isn't very hot, I'm afraid.'

Alexander obviously needed the refreshment as he gulped it down. Then he said, 'William and I may not get back home until late this evening. I'm going to ring your grandparents and ask them to have you two for the night — '

'No, no, no, Dad! Granny Joan is so strict.'

'Horrible!' Toby shouted. 'Jenny will look after us, won't you Jenny?'

Well . . . she could, couldn't she? Call for a taxi to take her home when Alexander got back from the hospital. She could see the dilemma Alexander was in. He had to find someone to look after his younger children while he escorted William to hospital — William was his child too, in pain and probably scared. He needed his dad by him.

Jenny took in a deep breath.

'OK. I will stay here until your father gets back.'

She almost fainted when she heard herself saying those words. Was she mad? Hadn't she already decided that there was no way she wanted to become involved with his family? She knew nothing about kids or cats or running a family house. She had already observed that his children were running rings around him — and she feared the cat might be pregnant, as she didn't suppose Belle had been neutered.

Oh dear! What had she let herself in for? Grandmother Joan didn't sound too nice, either!

But looking at Alexander, she knew she'd made the right decision. He needed her. It was getting dark now and he ought to head off to the hospital.

'I'm sorry, Jenny, to put you in this mess.'

'You haven't! It was an accident. The children and I will be fine until you get home. Don't worry about us. We'll manage.'

'Are you sure you don't mind?'

Jenny nodded and was delighted to see some of the worry clear from his face. 'I'll ring Cyril and Joan and let them know not to come, then.'

'Goody!' said Katie, clapping her hands.

Jenny pursed her lips. What a little madam she was! But very sweet too. A darling little girl who had lost her mama and needed another.

'At least it's Sunday tomorrow so there'll be no rush,' Alexander said, attempting to smile. Looking directly into Jenny's eyes, he added, 'I'll get back as soon as I can. You'll find Polly's parents' phone number in the hall phone book should you need to contact them.'

She tried to give him a reassuring smile. She had many questions, but knowing he had to dash away she kept her mouth shut.

No, she wasn't breaking her resolve not to become his housekeeper. This was an emergency, just as it had been when William had got lost coming home from school.

She'd been caught up in it.

The fact that she'd found a man she really liked was unfortunate — because there was no way she wanted to take on all the baggage he was carrying too.

Quickly Alexander bent down to kiss his youngest children, muttering, 'Be nice to Jenny,' and they nodded.

With a final lingering meeting of their eyes Jenny knew he was loath to leave her.

Moments later as the front door slammed Jenny knew she was on her own. Holding the fort.

★ ★ ★

Where the time went, Jenny just didn't know, but putting two young children to bed was entertainment enough. They demanded this and that, as if they were used to a routine, and if she cooperated — which she did — all went well.

Eventually when all went quiet — each child asleep in their own room, Jenny undertook a last tidy-up and went downstairs for a well-earned coffee.

The house had obviously been well organised by Alexander's wife. Now there was shambles. In the linen cupboard for example, bundles of clothes had been shoved in unfolded — and to her, what belonged to each member of the family was unfathom-able. She had the urge to tidy it — but what was the use? It would soon be back in the same state even if she tried!

Not that Alexander was a slovenly man; indeed she had the impression he was doing what he could to manage his family. And having other people, like his in-laws, to help him wasn't easy. Even the children seemed to resent their intrusion into their lives.

Still, she thought as she kicked off her shoes and put he feet up on the sofa in the sitting room, and sipped her coffee, that wasn't her problem.

Alexander was not short of money; he just had to find the best help to run his family home and it was early days yet. In time she was sure he would.

William's escapades were not help-ing, of course, but she had to remember how devasted that young man was after losing his mother. And being told by his maternal grandparents that he was not welcome at their home, which Alex-ander had explained to her was the case, didn't help him adjust either.

In some ways, she wanted to stay here. She seemed to belong, in some strange way. She seemed to fit into the family — even though she'd only been here for a few hours.

But she couldn't. She had to make her own new life — a life she chose, not one thrown at her. No matter how urgently Alexander needed someone to replace his lost wife.

She dozed off on the sofa in front of the fire, with Belle snuggled up to her.

★　★　★

The sound of the front door being opened and shut and footsteps coming into the room startled her. Oh no — what time was it?

The room lights were snapped on and Alexander looked surprised to see her.

'I thought you'd have taken a taxi home,' he said brusquely.

Raising herself and putting her

stockinged feet on the carpet, Jenny blinked at him.

'I couldn't leave the children, could I?' she said almost angrily.

He ran his fingers through his hair.

'Didn't Joan and Cyril turn up? I rang them from the hospital when I knew I was going to be late.'

Did he really think that they would? At this time of night, older people usually retired. He was just making a feeble excuse.

She swallowed. What was the point of her being dissatisfied? She knew she'd done a good job putting Katie and Toby to bed, but her work wasn't finished yet, as their father looked half dead on his feet. He needed to be looked after too — she should concentrate on that.

Having had a short sleep, Jenny felt refreshed. Standing up she said briskly, 'Go and wash your hands. I'll make some tea. I put a baked potato in the oven for you.'

Alexander blinked at her. 'I've got to

get you home first. Have you ordered a taxi?'

Once again, she doubted he really thought she would have. He was so tired he was not thinking logically, she decided.

'How's William?' she asked as she brushed by him on the way to the kitchen.

'William is going to be fine. My brother set his arm and arranged for him to stay overnight in the hospital.'

'That's good,' Jenny called out over the splash of water as she filled the kettle.

Belle weaved around her feet so the next thing she did was to give the cat more food, while Alexander washed his hands and slumped down on a kitchen chair. Before he had the chance to fall asleep, she'd plonked in front of him a plate with a hot, buttery baked potato. A tin of baked beans didn't take long to heat to add to his meal, which he ate almost automatically.

She wondered what would happen if

he fell asleep, as she couldn't help him upstairs.

However the food seemed to revive him.

'Look, Jenny. I'm terribly sorry about all this.'

Jenny refilled his teacup and sloshed some milk in it saying, 'Heavens, Alexander, it wasn't your fault! It's like all accidents, it just happened. Now hopefully all is well. William will recover. So go to bed. I'll sleep a bit more on the sofa, then I'll get a taxi tomorrow morning.'

He looked confused. Alexander wasn't like Marvin who'd made demands on her. She felt safe with him, so she added quickly, 'Just ring your mum and tell her I won't be in tonight in case she's concerned.'

'Jenny,' he said slowly as if trying to come to terms with what she'd said, 'I appreciate more than I can say what you are doing for us.'

'Go to bed!'

'OK. I am exhausted.' As he grabbed

hold of the door handle he gave the order, 'Now, you are to sleep in the master bedroom. I will sleep in William's room.'

Jenny retorted, 'If you can get in there. I glanced in his room as I put the little ones to bed, and it's chaotic! A real junk hole!'

Groaning he admitted, 'I know. I know. I just don't seem to be able to get through to William that he should clean it up.'

She saw him totter as though he might fall, so she darted towards him and pushed him out of the kitchen saying, 'It's Sunday tomorrow so you can have a lie-in. I'll see to the kids.'

It was quiet after he'd gone.

Finishing her night-time drink and looking around the kitchen Jenny thought of what was needed to feed the family in the next few days. Her eyes alighted on the kitchen clock. It was half-past eleven. If she was quick about it, she might just be able to order some groceries to be delivered tomorrow.

She fished her mobile out of her pocket and found the website of the store which the items in the kitchen cupboards indicated the family used. With minutes to spare, she was able to get a delivery at seven-thirty next day, and hurriedly tapped in the names of the first items she thought of. Practically every suggestion that popped up on the screen was something she had noticed needed replenishing. Her weekly shops were tiny compared to what a family needed. She blinked as the bill mounted up.

Whew! She breathed a sigh of relief when she got the confirmation back that the basic foodstuffs and cleaning materials — plus cat food — would be delivered in the early morning.

Worn out herself, Jenny didn't give any thought to the impropriety of staying overnight sleeping on his bed as he'd suggested. Not hearing Alexander, she went upstairs and, finding all the doors shut, hoped the door she opened would be the master bedroom. He'd been in there because the light in the en-suite was on, she presumed he'd popped in to collect a few things and left it on.

The double bed was comfortable and after setting the clock alarm for six-thirty, Jenny sank down and had no difficulty getting to sleep.

★   ★   ★

The next thing she was aware of was noises which made her wonder where she was.

The alarm hadn't worked!

Putting her thoughts in order, she realised the family were probably up and had left her to sleep. The faint smell of bacon told her firstly that the groceries she'd ordered last night had arrived, and secondly that Alexander was cooking breakfast in the way his children had told her he normally did at weekends.

Scampering outside her door and hushed voices told her the children were excited to think she was still in the house. She should get up.

The en-suite shower was soon running and she was standing under the refreshing spray.

Why shouldn't she make use of the personal toiletries that Polly had left in the bathroom and in the bedroom? She found what she needed and used it. Polly obviously had had beautiful red hair, like William, and her clothes — especially some colours — would not have been Jenny's choice.

Washed and dressed, she ventured out and almost bumped into the tall figure carrying a tray.

'Morning Jenny. I've brought you a cup of tea,' Alexander said, bending over to give her a quick kiss on her cheek.

His brief kiss sent a pleasant sensation all through her. A pinkness covered her cheeks as she remembered she mustn't encourage him to regard her as a member of his family, so she commented tartly, 'Thank you. *Most* of the tea I'll be able to enjoy,' looking pointedly at the spilled tea swilling round in the cup's saucer.

She felt awkward, their relationship uncertain. His face showed the strain he had been suffering recently, and the effort it must have been for him to get up early after William's escapade yesterday. He was, she thought, trying to keep his troubles to himself.

Just as he had spotted when she was in trouble with her knee, before her operation, and helped her, so she wanted to help him now. But that didn't mean staying here forever.

Adopting a less intimate tone, he said, 'Thank you for ordering the essential groceries for us last night, Jenny. That was brilliant of you to think of it. I usually have to do a huge supermarket shop on a Sunday to feed the kids for a week. Now I won't need to, and it's a relief. Let me know how much I owe you.'

'Forget it.'

He protested, 'It's my family's food

and I'm well able to pay for it. You are a guest here.'

'Alexander. Don't let's quarrel about the payment. I ordered it and it's all paid for. You know about my circumstances so just forget about it.'

In a conspiratorial voice, she added, 'Just don't tell the children I'm loaded!'

He replied quietly, 'We agreed about that some time ago! Don't keep bringing it up!'

She sensed he was annoyed she had, and could have kicked herself as he went on, 'I said I won't tell them.'

'Sorry.' She looked down at her feet. What else could she say to soothe his feelings about her fortune? It was getting in the way of their relationship and it shouldn't.

He blurted out, 'You are not to give us any more expensive presents.'

Oh dear, he was furious! Lost for words, she nodded meekly.

They were in agreement and she was glad about that. But the awkwardness between them remained. Perhaps it always would, she thought miserably.

It wasn't his fault that she'd been obliged to stay the night. But she had to continue to make it clear that she wasn't a permanent fixture in his home. And he had to accept that she didn't think he was after her fortune. But it clearly came between them — especially when the children were around. Fortunately, Jenny was used to leading a very simple life until recently. She had no intention of adopting a luxurious lifestyle.

'Let's go down and I'll throw out this tea and make you a better cup — or do you like coffee at breakfast time?'

Stepping in front of him as he politely suggested she should, Jenny walked easily downstairs realising with pleasure that her new knee wasn't giving her any pain.

'How's William?' she asked.

Reaching the kitchen, she was pleased to note there were no dirty dishes lying about and the cat had food and water in her bowls.

'William is OK. Sore, of course, but Jim is going to check his arm before he brings him home.'

'Your lordly brother is bringing William home?'

'Yep. And he's bringing another cat flap for the kitchen door. We are going to install it.'

'Wow! I didn't think your brother would do that!'

'I don't suppose he will. I will have to do it. He'll just hold the tools and give me a lot of advice!'

Bacon was already sizzling in the pan. Alexander held an egg up, asking, 'How do you like this cooked?'

He was a dab hand at a fry-up, and a nicely presented cooked breakfast was placed in front of her as she poured coffee. Strangely she didn't have to ask if he wanted any — she just seemed to know he did. In fact, he relished it, murmuring that she made coffee like Polly used to.

Not liking to think that she fitted too neatly into Polly's shoes, Jenny asked,

'Where are the little ones?'

'Outside. Building a tree house.'

Enjoying her cooked breakfast, Jenny thought there was no way she could scoot off and leave the family today. They would all be hungry by lunchtime and would need a good meal. She had ordered a joint she could put in the oven, potatoes she could roast, and various vegetables as she wasn't sure what the kids would eat. Then they would need a pudding on this crisply cold autumn day.

★　★　★

Surgeon Jim Sharman drove his nephew home and Jenny could tell that his uncle wouldn't take any nonsense from the lad. With his red hair and freckles standing out against his white face, his features morose, Jenny was glad Alexander didn't have to cope with the injured boy alone.

Uncle Jim was charming to her — so much so that Alexander scowled to see how Jenny responded to him. Was Alexander jealous that his elder brother could make Jenny giggle and obviously enjoy his company?

Katie had come in to help her with the cooking and the little girl was surprisingly useful as they chatted happily, preparing the vegetables and the pudding. Jenny suspected Katie had assisted her mother, and was happy to help Jenny too.

Jenny was amused to hear the way the brothers teased one another as they took off the kitchen door and made a hole in it for the cat flap. Their laughter showed they weren't quite as unfriendly as their exchanges suggested.

When the men had finished they went into the sitting room for a chat and a pre-lunch drink and little Toby spent time teaching Belle, the cat, how to use the new flap. Jenny noticed William helping too, which thrilled her.

Jenny had to admit the joint — which had been a very good offer on the internet — was a great success, making a splendid family Sunday meal. When Jenny had eaten her roast potato and looked to take another, the whole large dishful had gone! The apple pie and custard didn't last very long either.

Uncle Jim ordered William up to his room to rest and said he wasn't to go back to school for a few days. Without protesting, William left the table. Prompted by his father, he thanked his uncle for mending his arm and bringing him home, and thanked Jenny for the meal. He grinned as he said that, as if he really did enjoy it.

Jim said he had to get back to the hospital to check on a few patients. The hug and kiss he gave Jenny as he thanked her was watched by Alexander, whose face showed clearly that he didn't like the easy way Jim had with her. Although Jenny's preference was for the widowed younger man, she found it difficult to show it. Or to say anything which showed that she did.

But oh, how she'd begun to fall for

the powerful, handsome brother surgeon too! His polished manners and obvious charm with the ladies enchanted her. He seemed to have all the self-confidence and leadership skills. No, he wasn't a bully like Marvin had tended to be. Jim was a caring man, a doctor who would go into the hospital on his day off, as he had today.

Jenny was pleased she'd given him a good Sunday roast with all the trimmings, and he was full of praise for her cooking.

Jim hadn't suggested that she should stay for a while, but Jenny felt sure he would wish her to. The family still needed her. It was nice to feel wanted. To have an important job to do. If she went back to her flat, she would only be worrying about the family when she was aware of all the jobs that needed doing here.

Making cold beef sandwiches for the evening meal, she took a plateful up to William.

The boy was playing a computer game with difficulty, using one hand, and jumped seeing her come into his room.

'How are you feeling, William?'

'Not bad.'

'Did your uncle suggest you took painkillers?'

'Yep.'

'I suggest you have them before your meal.'

She looked around and saw a glass of water with two tablets on a saucer by it. He had not been left with the packet of painkillers — only a dose. Jenny thought that was wise not to allow the boy access to them. He was still suffering from shock as well as some pain.

Of more concern to her was his state of mind. His father was, understandably, angry with him for causing the accident, but Alexander wasn't a hard-hearted father. It was, as Jenny saw it, a confrontation between a loving father and his wayward teenage son.

She could help both the injured boy and his distraught dad — but that, she suddenly realised, meant she had to stay the night again.

9

Downstairs Jenny found Alexander stretched out on the sofa.

On hearing her come into the sitting room, he swung his feet down and rather shakily stood up.

Obviously exhausted — she wasn't surprised after what had happened to him in the last forty-eight hours — he made the effort to greet her pleasantly.

'Jenny. Thank you for all you've done today . . . '

His voice petered out as he seemed unable to say, or even remember, what he wanted to thank her for.

She smiled back at him, thinking that would make him understand that she, too, thought the day had gone well.

She looked with sympathy at his worn expression of sheer tiredness.

'I left you a cold beef sandwich in the

kitchen — under cover so the cat didn't eat it.'

His eyes showed a spark of interest.

'I am hungry,' he confessed. He took a step forward, but she put up her hand to halt him.

'Stay there. I'll get the tray and bring it. You might fall over in the shaky state you're in.'

Why had she said that? Whether it was the way she was getting used to giving orders or because he thought he might not be able to stagger to the kitchen, Jenny wasn't sure.

Returning with the loaded tray, she wondered if he would still be awake.

He was! Even the short nap he'd had seemed to have refreshed him. She moved a small table towards the sofa and sat down near him.

'These sandwiches are delicious,' he said indistinctly, munching them. She smiled.

'The horseradish sauce adds flavour nicely. But it was a good joint — on offer online, so I'm glad I ordered it as all the family seemed to enjoy their Sunday lunch.'

They didn't say anything for a while, just ate and then sipped their coffee.

She took his mug when it seemed in danger of slipping out of his hands. He awoke with a cry.

'I ought to go and make sure the bonfire is out,' he muttered. 'Toby was in the garden before lunch, building his tree house, and he may have got it going again.'

'Not now. You're to stay here.'

Jenny put all the supper things on the tray. Then she found he had taken her hand, smoothed it and pressed his lips gently on her wrist.

His touch was magical. The sensation of his large hand covering hers sent exciting stabs of pleasure though her body. She wanted to push his hair from his forehead so that she could kiss him. On his lips too.

She resisted. How easy it would be to show her love for him physically.

But she knew she shouldn't. Not this

evening when he was tired. Because the gentle overtures to making love could so easily turn to passion.

Not that she could see any reason why they shouldn't make love . . .

Yes, she could! She wasn't prepared to allow herself — her decision to stay with him and his family — to be based on sexual desire.

Maybe one day she would change her mind. But not now.

Alexander had drifted off to sleep again. So Jenny got up, lifted his feet onto the sofa where she'd been sitting, and taking the supper tray went quietly out of the room.

In the kitchen she did a quick tidy-up and checked for any sign of bonfire smoke at the far end of the garden. Nothing.

The cat was given fresh water and some extra food, although Belle didn't turn a hair as she was curled up in her basket, snoring gently.

Turning off the lights downstairs, she went up to Alexander's bedroom.

A quick, motherly glance at the children in their rooms showed all three were dead to the world.

Having no embarrassment about using a few of Polly's things, because she felt sure Polly would approve of her looking after her husband and children, Jenny went to bed.

It had been another eventful day. A successful day. A happy day for her, looking after the family, feeding them. Working in Polly's kitchen had been a pleasure. The children were fun to be with and showed they approved of her — which was a blessing.

How she would be able to say goodbye to them all in the morning just didn't bear thinking about.

However, Jenny was someone who believed in enjoying the sunshine in one's life whenever the clouds parted. Maybe this phase in her life would pass without angst. She would be able to look back and think she had been able to help this family at a difficult time.

However her future would take a turn

that she hadn't anticipated.

She was almost asleep as her head touched the pillow, not even giving a thought to setting the alarm for an early wake-up call.

★ ★ ★

Jenny must have woken up and, feeling she needed more sleep, dozed off again. A little later she had the impression the bedroom door had opened and closed again.

Turning to look at her clock, she blinked. It couldn't be almost ten in the morning! Yet her closed curtains were keeping out the daylight.

For a moment or two she struggled to think where she was. In Alexander's bed! The first thing that came into her mind was to get up, washed and go down and see what needed doing.

It was Monday morning. Alexander must have got up and gone to work and the children must have gone to school. Except for William, whom she seemed to remember was told to rest for a few days after his accident and operation — so it must be him she had heard downstairs.

Barefoot she went to the door and listened.

She was sure someone was in the house. Sounds could be heard downstairs. But no children's voices.

In her present state of undress, she didn't feel like calling out to find out who it was.

Diving back into the bedroom, she rushed into the shower.

Having none of her own with her, she searched the drawers to find some clean underclothes — fortunately Polly's fitted her. Hurriedly she brushed her hair and tried to make her now rather crumpled shirt look tidy.

Then she trotted downstairs, expecting to find William in the kitchen. Instead a stout woman with a thunderous-looking face was sitting there!

'Oh — hello!' Jenny made the effort to give the lady a polite smile. Getting no reply, she asked, 'Who are you?'

With eyes like glaring searchlights, the woman retorted, 'I'm Mrs Davies, if you must know.' The lady evidently felt she had every right to be there — and Jenny didn't.

Ignoring the rebuff, because Jenny thought she might be the cleaner who wouldn't know who she was, Jenny said, 'I'm Jenny Warner. Where is everyone?'

'Mr Sharman has gone to work. A long time ago.'

'And the children?'

'At school. Although William is upstairs in bed.'

Wondering again if this this woman was the cleaner — although there were no signs of her rolling her sleeves up and starting work — Jenny asked, 'Is William OK?'

'I don't know if he is or not. I'm not going to find out. He's a hooligan!'

Jenny had to chuckle. 'Yes, well I agree William's not exactly a docile boy, but he is only twelve years old and is suffering from a broken arm that needs time to heal, so he needs looking after. Has he had some breakfast?'

'I'm not waiting on him!'

'You don't have to — I will.'

Jenny made to fill the kettle but it was a little difficult as Mrs Davies was sitting on a kitchen chair in front of it.

'Excuse me,' she said, 'I'll make some tea. Would you like some?'

Not budging an inch, the woman suddenly put her hands over her face and to Jenny's horror began to sob.

Was she worried that Jenny was taking over the house and would give her the sack? Surely not!

Whatever the reason, Jenny's reaction was instinctive. She put her arm around the woman's shoulders and tried to comfort her.

'There, there,' she said. 'I expect you are upset because I'm here. But don't be. I only came to visit the family on Saturday, then got caught up with helping out. I'm sure you know this house better than I do.'

'You don't understand.' Mrs Davies continued to sob, although she did shift herself enough for Jenny to grab the kettle and fill it to make the tea.

Why was she making such a fuss? Why was she so upset? Jenny hadn't done anything. Perhaps she was worried about losing her job? Perhaps she'd been asked to look after William and didn't like him? Perhaps William had been rude to her?

'When we've had some tea,' Jenny said remembering where the tea caddy was, and grabbing the teapot, 'you'll feel better.'

'No. I will not! This is my daughter's kitchen and she isn't here.'

The awful truth dawned on Jenny. This lady was Alexander's mother-in-law, Mrs Joan Davies, the children's grandmother they didn't like very much. And Jenny had spent the night in her daughter's bed and was wearing her daughter's deodorant and underclothes! No wonder Joan was so upset.

It wasn't many months ago that Polly

was in this kitchen. Joan would see her as a usurper. How could she explain that she hadn't slept with her daughter's husband, when Joan had probably seen her asleep in his bed?

With a deep sigh Jenny walked to the window and looked out. It was a damp and dreary autumn morning.

What could she say? How should she explain the reason she'd slept in Alexander's bed? And heaven knows where he'd spent the night.

She baulked at the idea of trying to tell Polly's mother that neither she, nor Alexander, had any intention of having an affair.

Jenny knew she felt attracted to Alexander. She knew he needed someone like her to take Polly's place in his life. Maybe he liked her. But Mrs Davies was not to know the reason why she didn't want to encourage any romance.

Nor could she hurriedly explain to Polly's mother how Alexander and she had met, and how she came to be here now. If Mrs Davies was upset, it was understandable — but why should Jenny apologise for a situation that wasn't her fault?

She sighed. If Polly's mother was less of a battleaxe, then it might be easier!

Then she noticed an envelope on the worktop by the toaster. *JENNY* was printed on it.

Opening it, she found a scribbled note from Alexander — obviously written in a great hurry.

Dear Jenny

I didn't like to wake you this morning as you needed the rest. I took Katie and Toby to a friend's house. Tracy will see they get to school this morning. They will go to their grandparents in the village after school.

William should rest today. I'm seeing his headmaster before I come home to arrange some schoolwork for him to do.

Rosie, our cleaner, should be coming this morning. She knows what to do.

I'll run you home this evening.

Alexander

Jenny breathed in relief as she saw he had organised everything — and hadn't written anything that Joan might interpret as indicating an attachment or affair between her and Alexander. Because she was sure Joan had read the note.

Jenny also felt sure he wouldn't have expected Joan to come barging in this morning — any more than she had.

But Jenny, being kind-hearted as Alexander was, didn't see the lady sitting opposite her as a great problem; she just felt very sorry for her. She hoped in time to convince her that there was nothing going on between Alexander and herself — she hadn't slept with him. Nor did she intend to.

Jenny knew she could now phone for a taxi and go home. Except that, no, she couldn't. Upstairs was a very volatile young man and downstairs a highly critical grandmother who might throttle him! She had to deal with the situation calmly.

She well understood the grief both were suffering because of Polly's death.

Jenny also understood that William was a gifted boy with a lot of potential. He'd won a scholarship to a top school. If he could be encouraged to behave, then the rift between him and his grandmother would heal just as his arm would. Suddenly Jenny saw her role as a referee, someone who could with luck do a useful job making sure the family were all as well-adjusted as possible before she left them.

Making the tea, she poured out two mugs and placed one on the table near Joan, remembering how that lovely nurse Sister Mary had treated her when she was set against having her knee operation. Cheerfully — just getting on with things.

'I'm so very sorry about your daughter's death, Mrs Davies, and I realise how difficult it must be for you to come here. Now, I'm going to make some breakfast for William and take it up to him.'

A bacon sandwich didn't take long to prepare. With that and another mug of tea on a tray, Jenny went upstairs, balanced the tray on the banister and knocked on William's door.

Getting no reply, she pushed open the door and went in. She wasn't surprised to see a mess everywhere — but she was surprised to see a boy armed with a cricket bat as if he was about to attack her!

'My goodness, William. I'm only bringing in your breakfast,' she said.

William's freckled face relaxed.

There was no room for a tray or anywhere to sit. But Jenny didn't grumble. She put the tray on the floor and sat at the end of his bed. Then she handed him his drink and sandwich, which he ate at speed. She was glad, as it showed he must be feeling better.

'Has she gone?' he asked, gulping his drink.

'If you mean your grandmother, no, she hasn't.'

'She doesn't like me!'

Jenny felt like retorting, *If you behave badly and are rude to her, are you surprised?* But she held her tongue. She wasn't going to take sides. Her job was to improve the relationship between William and his grandmother. Something she was sure his mother, Polly, would want. Polly must have loved her mother and she would have wanted her son to do so, too.

But Jenny knew it was necessary for her to tackle the problem sensitively, without sounding critical so she looked at the bandaged splint on his arm and asked, 'How's your arm today, William?'

The boy shrugged. 'So-so.'

It must be uncomfortable for him but she wanted to be supportive and cheer him up. She asked, 'Have you tried out the new mobile I gave you?'

A flash of anger showed his frustration.

'I can't use it can I?'

'Why not?'

'Because my right hand is out of action.'

'Well, learn to use it with your uninjured hand. Where is it?'

Jenny was gratified to see William had put the phone, still in its wrapping paper, under his pillow. She guessed he had chosen to put it there because he valued it.

For the next half-hour she assisted William by preparing it for use, using her own phone to register it and download some of the apps he wanted. He was clumsy at first but soon began to master using it one-handed. Jenny smiled to see the boy's confidence grow and his mood improve.

'Gracious! I'd better get downstairs and prepare the lunch,' Jenny said looking at her watch. 'What would you like to eat?'

Engrossed, William didn't reply.

Jenny snapped at him,

'William, I can see you are delighted with your new phone. But to thank me for it, you should make the effort to be considerate to others. I asked you what you wanted me to get you for lunch. I expect you to answer me.'

The boy coloured and looked up.

'Oh yes — thank you, Jenny. I like shepherd's pie.'

'OK. I'll make one. You have half an hour before you should come downstairs. I dare say Rosie, your cleaner, has arrived and she will want to tidy up a bit so that she can clean your room.'

He grinned. 'Rosie has given up on my room.'

'No, she hasn't. I'll take down a tray of your empty mugs, plates and rubbish. You, young man, will pick your clothes up, put things away and greet Rosie with a smile when she comes to strip your bedclothes to put in the wash.'

William, eyeing the clothes strewn about, looked doubtful.

'I can't do it with my arm out of action, can I?'

Jenny laughed triumphantly. 'If you

can use your smartphone, you can tidy up.'

She wanted to add that he should remember to be polite to his grandmother, but didn't know if she was still in the house. She certainly didn't want to dictate to William about good manners — especially as his grandmother may say something to antagonise him.

Jenny had difficulty getting downstairs with the heavy tray load. But she managed, and went into the kitchen to find two ladies there.

Rosie, Alexander's cleaning lady, had arrived and the women were chatting earnestly. It wasn't difficult for Jenny to work out that she was the subject of their conversation.

Jenny was obviously the scarlet woman in the dock! The woman whom Joan had found in Alexander's bed that morning.

While Joan was still looking censorious, Rosie looked gobsmacked. She was a cuddly, older woman dressed in an overall and holding a basket of household cleaning materials.

'Hello,' Jenny said cheerfully, refusing to allow their hostile stares to intimidate her. She had to allow that until recently Joan had been feeling at home in her daughter's house, and the cleaner may be wondering if she would be replaced by Mr Sharman's new woman — herself.

As they stared open-mouthed, Jenny came in and put down the piled-up tray.

'I've brought this down from William's room, but I dare say there is more to be cleared away. He has been told that his room is to be blitzed. So, in a while we can go up and collect his washing and bedding to be put in the washing machine.'

As neither of the ladies made a comment, Jenny said, 'I'm going to make lunch. William wants me to make a shepherd's pie.'

'Oh, does he!' Joan almost shouted.

'Yes, he does!' Jenny retorted. 'He is

still recovering from his accident, and his uncle, who is a surgeon, says he has to be looked after and have time to recover.'

Joan nodded. At least she agreed with that.

Jenny continued, 'In fact I need to make two pies. One for William now, and one for the family for their supper. That means I have to peel some onions and lots of potatoes and carrots — which I will find in the vegetable rack because I put them there.'

'Are you the new cook?' Rosie ventured.

'I'm the dogsbody,' she announced, going to the door to get Polly's apron which she put on.

Her choice of calling herself the woman available for doing anything was perhaps not wise as it didn't remove the older ladies' suspicion that she was also Alexander's bedfellow. But she was soon far too busy peeling and chopping the vegetables and lightly frying the onions and mince in a pan on the hob to think about anything other than cooking.

While Jenny was busy, Rosie went off to begin her cleaning jobs. Joan sat for a while brooding. At least she wasn't preventing Jenny from cooking.

Rosie came back dragging a huge bundle of washing which she sorted into four loads, then shoved the first into the large machine, which was soon whirring away.

'Let's have some coffee,' suggested Jenny.

To her surprise, Joan got up and proceeded to make it. Brilliant! At least having something to do would prevent Polly's mother from sitting and agonising about her loss.

'The biscuit tin is empty!' Joan complained.

'Yes,' Jenny agreed. 'I didn't get any because I make cakes and biscuits. Much healthier. I think there are still a few flapjacks I made yesterday in the cupboard. Would you like to try one?'

Joan went to the store cupboard and

found the plate. Taking a cautious bite, she exclaimed, 'These flapjacks are delicious! I am amazed they haven't all been eaten.'

Jenny grinned. That was purely because she'd hidden them in the cupboard.

Rosie was glad to sit down for a rest and informed Jenny she'd been cleaning the sitting room, taking the ash from the grate, and then dealing with all the bedlinen.

Sipping her coffee Jenny was suddenly aware that Belle, the cat, was meowing as she was curling around her feet.

Joan blinked. 'That's Polly's cat!'

'Yes,' said Jenny. 'Mrs Sharman, Alexander's mother, has been looking after her, but the family wanted her back home.'

Jenny got up to feed the beautiful Siamese.

'She looks as though she's eaten too many biscuits already!' commented Joan.

Jenny wanted to ask if Belle had been neutered — but dare not. She suspected Alexander hadn't got around to that. She would have to remind him to take the cat to the vet. With the cat munching happily and everyone enjoying their coffee break it seemed best to avoid any contentious subjects.

'Shall I make some jam tarts?' Joan asked suddenly. Her pleading look almost broke Jenny's heart. The poor lady was suffering from acute grief after losing her beloved daughter and seeing another woman in her place. Yet she had made the effort to help the family.

Jenny beamed and touched Joan's hand.

'Oh! Thank you, Joan. That would be lovely,' she said, looking into the older lady's troubled eyes.

'I made some jam last year and gave Polly some,' Joan said, rising and going to a wall cupboard. 'Which jam shall I use?'

Joan's confidence seemed to have vanished.

'I'm sure Katie would like some red ones,' suggested Jenny.

'Ah, yes, you are right,' Joan agreed.

Pastry-making, rolling out and then cutting to fit the tins occupied the two women as the shepherd's pies were finished and one put in the oven for lunch.

Rosie finished her cleaning, put the washing in the dryer, and reloaded the washing machine.

It pleased Jenny to find the antagonism she'd suffered had evaporated.

All was going well until a sudden scream came from upstairs.

Jenny flew up as fast as she could to William's room. What on earth had the boy done now?

10

Bursting into William's room, Jenny found him standing looking out of the window with his mobile phone in his hand.

All the colour seemed to have drained out of his face as he pointed out of the window.

At the far end of the garden Jenny, aghast, saw a tree alight! Flames were leaping and smoke was billowing into the air.

She was aware of William saying between sobs, 'It's the bonfire. I didn't put it out properly. It's my fault. Dad's shed has caught alight too. All his tools will be burned! There was petrol, too, for his new sit-on lawn mower which he needs for our field grass.'

Jenny was appalled. For once she was at loss what to do.

Then she heard William's voice. 'I've

called for the Fire Brigade.'

They looked at each other open-mouthed, as tears filled their eyes.

What could they do? Both of them were recovering from operations. Jenny had a replacement knee that prevented her from running out into the garden — and what would she do if she did? Carry a bucket of water down the garden to try and put out a huge blazing tree? William wouldn't even be able to fill and carry a pail of water!

But he *had* had the sense to call for the fire brigade.

Jenny judged that the fire was too far away from the house for it to catch alight — she hoped.

Then she thought of Joan in the kitchen baking the jam tarts. What kind of a state would she be in when she heard the fire engine siren and became aware of the fire?

'William,' she managed to say. 'We will have to leave the fire for the firemen to put out. But I think you have been very clever to call for the fire brigade to come and we can only hope they will be here very soon.'

'There is a fire station in our nearest town — where we go shopping. It shouldn't take the crew long to reach us. They are always on standby for an emergency.'

'How sensible you are, William. Now I want you to be just as grown-up dealing with your grandmother downstairs. She will be frightened and you must reassure her as I will try and do.'

William nodded. He didn't argue, although he still looked miserable even as Jenny praised him. She was sure he would prefer to go out into the garden to await the fire crew and then see the fire being extinguished. Exciting for a young lad to have that drama to watch.

He was still distressed and thinking the fire was his fault, as he told her going downstairs. 'I was the last person to check that the bonfire had gone out — and I didn't do it properly, did I?'

Jenny was only concerned about

putting the damn fire out, and didn't reply as she huffed and puffed to get downstairs quickly. Her knee, so much better since the operation, was beginning to complain with all the running up and down.

It was just as well the younger children were not back from school yet. She didn't have to worry about their safety. And the cat could use the cat-flap to get away.

Coming into the kitchen, Jenny saw Joan peering out at the smoke outside and remarked that she hoped the oven where her tarts and the shepherd's pie were cooking was not faulty. On noticing William running outside into the garden, she turned to Jenny and said, 'What's that wretched boy up to now?'

'Joan, William noticed a fire in the garden, which he thinks is the bonfire flaring up again. He's been very sensible and has called the fire brigade, which should be arriving soon.'

The expression on Jenny's face was

enough to tell Joan that the situation was not a joke.

'We can stay in the house,' Jenny continued breathlessly. 'The fire is right down the bottom of the garden and shouldn't be a danger to us.' Jenny tried to sound reassuring, although her heart was pumping wildly.

Joan looked out of the patio door window and saw the tree ablaze, behind the hedge. She was too overcome to speak and covered her mouth with her hands.

Putting her arm around Joan, Jenny moved a dining chair so that Joan could sit on one.

'We will keep an eye on things and be ready to make a run for it in case the fire does come this way.'

Fortunately, Joan didn't panic and sat with Jenny watching the inferno outside. The breeze blew the smoke around and added to the drama going on.

Jenny was concerned for William's safety.

'I do hope William doesn't try to put

the fire out,' she muttered.

'There is an outside tap and a hose Polly used to water her plants — but I doubt if it would reach that far down the garden,' said Joan.

Shortly a small figure could be seen coming towards the house through the smoke and swirling ash particles. It was William, staggering to the house, and despite fearing the smoke would come billowing in, Jenny opened the patio window and pulled him inside.

He was coughing and covered with white ash. He was crying, and Jenny was pleased to see his granny putting her arm around him and pushing his now-white hair from his face.

'I'm glad you've had the sense to come back here,' Joan said. 'It was too dangerous for you to stay by the fire. And I understand you had the sense to call for the fire brigade and they will know how to deal with it.'

Meanwhile Jenny had got him a mug of water which William sipped. But as soon as he was able to say anything, he spluttered, 'It's my fault. I should have put the bonfire out.'

To that statement, Joan said nothing. Jenny was glad she didn't as William was shivering and she feared the sick boy had tried to get things out of the shed and may have injured his arm.

'Dad's mower is alight,' sobbed William. 'I couldn't move it.'

Jenny, who knew she could easily afford to replace any machinery or garden tools or equipment and the shed Alexander may have lost, was not able to reassure William that he must not worry about that. The children and Joan would not be aware she was a millionaire, and this was not the time to tell them.

This was a precious time though as it became clear to Jenny that William and his grandmother were not as antagonistic towards each other as she'd been led to believe. Joan was trying to comfort him as his mother would have done. And William, full of remorse, was trying to apologise.

It was a touching sight, seeing William and Joan with their arms around each other, and Jenny thought it was a pity Alexander wasn't there to see it.

The blaring sound of the fire engine and sounds of men shouting and running outside announced the arrival of the fire brigade. William eased himself out of Joan's embrace saying he wanted to go out and see them.

'Let him go,' Jenny said. 'The firefighters will be there to look after him.'

*   *   *

Alexander felt William's headmaster was being remarkably sympathetic towards William.

'He is a very intelligent boy, is William. As you have requested, my staff have assembled some homework for him to do so that he doesn't get behind in his studies. But I appreciate that having lost his mother recently and then being bullied by some bigger boys from another school — then breaking his arm — is a lot for him to cope with.'

'Yes.' Alexander nodded.

'And the toll has been heavy for you, too.'

Miserably Alexander agreed again.

The headmaster continued, 'You have other children too, I think, Mr Sharman.'

'Yes, two younger ones.'

'Any relatives to help you?'

Alexander thought of Polly's parents and almost told the headmaster what he thought of them — especially their dislike of William. But he merely said they had been helpful. His mind turned to thinking about Jenny, who he wondered about. Was she waiting for him to take her home, as he had suggested in the note he had left her? Or had she already taken a taxi back to town?

If so, he and his family would miss her.

How Alexander wished she was not

loaded with money and he was on an equal footing with her. Then he could ask her to marry him. But he had no intention of being labelled a fortune-seeker.

Anyway, she hadn't suggested it. Nor had she shown any signs of wanting an amorous relationship with him. He suspected she had the same feelings about him as he had about her, but they were both holding back.

It was very soon after Polly's death — and being saddled with three stepchildren was hardly what a bride would want — especially William for one!

Then looking at his watch, he said, 'I must be off. It's time for me to collect the children and prepare supper. Thank you for your help.'

He stood and picked up a notebook with the pile of books for William to study.

A sharp rap on the door was followed by the entrance of the school secretary who said, 'There is an urgent call for

Mr Sharman to ring his home number.'
She then disappeared.

The headmaster suggested he used his mobile.

Alexander's face turned grey as he ran his fingers through his thick hair. 'Oh no!' he cried.

'What's the matter, Mr Sharman?'

Alexander's eyes closed as he answered in distress, 'There's been a fire at my house!'

'Anyone hurt?'

'No, fortunately the fire brigade came and put it out. But I must get home straight away.'

★ ★ ★

Mercifully Alexander's dash home took place before the rush hour began in earnest. He arrived to find his way blocked by a fire engine. Leaving his car rammed up against a hedge, he sprang out and tore into his front drive almost colliding with a firefighter.

'Whoa!' exclaimed the man, rolling

up a flattened hose. 'No need to panic, sir. The fire is out.'

'What caused it?' panted Alexander.

'A bonfire, sir. Not extinguished properly.'

'But I did put it out!' As if he had been hit by a thunderbolt, Alexander reeled.

'Bonfires can smoulder for days. There has been no rain for a week and a strong breeze can whip up a flame in a dying fire very easily.'

Yes, thought Alexander, *and I should have checked it this morning before I went to work* — but he knew he'd been too tired. Too exhausted after William's accident, and having to sleep on the sofa as Jenny was occupying his bed.

He turned his eyes to the distant apple tree which was a skeleton against the sky.

'My shed?'

The fireman shook his head. 'It was already alight when we arrived, sir. Couldn't save anything — burned to a cinder. I hope you have some insurance for the contents.'

Alexander raced down the garden to see for himself the scale of the disaster.

Sodden grey ash heaps and burned timbers were all that remained of the new shed he had built himself. The new sit-on mower he'd saved up to buy was a smouldering heap of scrap, and his garden tools were all charred and shrivelled.

He found he couldn't hold back his tears. Standing behind the hedge — which fortunately hadn't caught fire — he wept in agony at seeing what the fire had done.

He was unaware of Jenny coming up — she'd seen him running down the garden and had followed him.

She slid her arms around him and said softly, 'Alexander. I am so sorry this happened.'

So many things she could say, but what was the use? For him, she knew this was only another blast of bad luck. He didn't deserve it. He was suffering deep anguish — as this disaster was yet another catastrophe to befall him. He was exhausted having been hit so many times recently, and she felt his pain — she was suffering with him.

He didn't apologise for crying, and why should he? He just put his arms around her and hugged her close. She was crying too — for him. It seemed natural for them to try and comfort each other.

She could have reminded him that she could replace everything he'd lost. But it was not tactful.

All she needed to do at present was to be there with him, to support him at this especially difficult time. To help him care for his children and run his household like a cook-cum-house-keeper — a job she liked doing anyway.

But she was also aware that she liked being held in his arms. That she wanted him to hold her forever.

How they came to kiss, Jenny was unsure. She was not surprised when his lips touched hers; it seemed a natural thing to have happened. After a brief caress, his lips demanded they kiss some more — and she responded.

But then she broke away. That was not right when they were not declared lovers. They had not discussed the problems she had about their future relationship, nor had he mentioned his reservations about her. She felt it was far too early after Polly's death for him to begin a romantic relationship. Possibly he felt that it would not be fair on her to burden her with mothering his three children.

But there were at present practical considerations. She couldn't expect him to run her home tonight — he was far too exhausted and needed a proper night's sleep. She would have to take a taxi back home.

Then reality hit her.

'The shepherd's pie!' she cried, thinking she should put it in the oven for the children's tea.

Puzzled, he asked, 'What did you say?'

She eased away from him and said, 'I

think we should go back and see what the children are up to — they should be back now. I need to put the pie I made for the family in the oven.'

He gave a great sigh as though he, too, must resume his duties. Jenny had enabled him to shoulder his disappointment at losing yet more in his life. She'd not made him feel embarrassed about showing his anger and sorrow. She seemed to understand him, just as Polly would have done.

But life had to go on, and he had to shrug off his wounds. Jenny had reminded him that his children needed him and he had to carry on looking after them, doing his best for them. They were not Jenny's responsibility — although he was sure she liked them.

They resisted walking arm in arm back to the house. It seemed both of them were unwilling to show their affection for each other, denying their embrace just now had ever happened.

Toby's small figure emerged from the kitchen patio door and he raced towards them shouting, 'Dad! Dad! William has locked himself in his room and won't come out. Katie and I have been banging on it and he told us to bugger off!'

Jenny caught hold of Alexander's sleeve as he looked as though he would run indoors. She suspected he was thinking of crashing into his son's room either by breaking the door lock or climbing in through his bedroom window. But his bedroom window was on a sheer wall and only an experienced window cleaner with the right ladder would attempt to reach it. Alexander wasn't. He was upset, tired and hurt himself.

'Alexander, please listen to me. William is upset because he thinks the fire was his fault. Now don't you go climbing a ladder to get to his bedroom window. You may fall!' She took a deep breath and added, 'I'll go up and talk to him.'

11

Persuading Alexander to look after his two younger children and put the pie in the oven, Jenny went upstairs and tapped firmly on William's door saying, 'It's only me. Let me in, please.'

There was no response.

Jenny called out, 'Your father isn't angry with you, William. He thinks the fire was his fault — he says he should have checked the bonfire before he went off to work this morning. In any case it was Toby who was there last, and he wouldn't have noticed the fire wasn't still smouldering.' She gulped and prayed William would accept her explanation of what had happened.

It sounded as though William had barricaded himself in his room as she heard the boy moving some furniture he'd put up against the door.

Then she heard the door being

unlocked and William's sad face appeared in the inch he allowed the door to open.

'Are you really sure?' was all he said.

'Sure I'm sure.' Jenny should know; she'd been in Alexander's arms a few minutes ago and trying to comfort him — only their affection for each other had led to a passionate kiss that had raised their relationship higher than mere friendship. 'Your dad is mad with himself for allowing the fire to happen so the best thing for you is to come down and make yourself useful.'

William considered this, then said almost angrily, 'What does he want me to do? I can't clear up the remains of the shed!'

Jenny gently eased herself into his room.

'Of course not! All you have to do is help him get the supper, perhaps have a game with your brother and sister before bedtime. It is a school day tomorrow so they should go to bed early.'

'Ugh! I don't play with them! Dad can do it.'

Jenny felt like shaking him.

'William! You are always thinking about yourself! Don't you realise that your father is doing his best for you all? He has taken the blame for the fire, hasn't he? Now he needs you to help him — '

Jenny checked her tongue. It was not her intention to make the lad feel guilty about the fire again. So she hurriedly went on to suggest, 'Toby was given a new electric railway set. It is not a simple toy. Grown-ups like to play with them! It won't hurt you — even with one arm in a sling — to set it up for him. After all, I helped you set up your mobile phone, didn't I?'

A sparkle showed in William's eyes.

'Oh, yes, you did. I dare say I could give Toby some advice to do that.'

'OK, then. We'll see you downstairs in a few minutes.'

In the kitchen Jenny was pleased to see Alexander, Katie and Toby tucking into the shepherd's pie and a place at the table laid for her.

Alexander rose to greet her, saying, 'We didn't know how long you'd be, Jenny. The pie smelled so delicious we couldn't wait to eat it.'

Jenny had to admit it did smell good. She sat in her place and Alexander took out the remains of the pie they had saved for her.

'You're a good cook, Jenny,' Toby said, taking the last of the gravy off his plate with his finger and licking it.

'Toby!' cried Alexander. 'Miss Warner hasn't given you permission to use her first name. And stop using your finger to mop up your plate.'

Jenny swallowed a mouthful and said, 'Alexander, I don't mind if the children call me Jenny.' She then turned to speak to Toby. 'When William comes in a minute and has eaten his supper, I hope he will offer to help you set up your new model railway, although it will be difficult for him with one arm.'

'I'll help,' said a male voice. Jenny

became aware of an elderly gentleman who'd come into the kitchen via the patio door.

No longer surprised by the people who kept appearing in this house, Jenny quickly finished her meal and began to prepare a supper for William who'd had his shepherd's pie at lunchtime.

'Jenny,' she heard Alexander say, 'meet Cyril, my father-in-law.'

Jenny turned with apprehension. Was he as prickly as his wife, Joan? She had a pleasant surprise on seeing twinkly eyes and a smile.

'Pleased to meet you,' Cyril said, coming forward and shaking her hand, 'I've been hearing a lot about you.'

I'm sure you have! Jenny remembered how his wife, Joan, had attacked her for being, as she'd thought, Alexander's bedfellow. And no doubt half the villagers now thought so too.

'I have been down to where the shed was, and I was telling Alexander that it can be rebuilt and I would be happy to help him.'

'That's kind of you,' murmured Jenny.

Cyril went on, 'Not at all. I'll enjoy the job — if Alexander doesn't mind having me around.'

'I'll be glad of your help, Cyril,' Alexander said quickly. 'You know where the local builders' yards are, and while I'm at work you can begin to organise the materials that'll be needed.'

This was all music to Jenny's ears. She hadn't a clue where to start building a shed. Cyril sounded — unlike his wife — as though he got on with Alexander. It was great to hear that the children had a supportive grandfather.

'I'm also a fan of Hornby train sets,' continued Cyril. 'I had one when I was about seven — the same age as Toby — when my hands were nimble enough to put the rails together.'

Thrilled to hear that her gift to Toby was going to be such a success, Jenny smiled broadly.

Toby crashed into the room and announced that he wanted some help, and taking his grandfather's hand pulled him out of the kitchen.

Alexander winked at Jenny.

'I'll go and get the camp bed down from the loft. I really don't think I should take you home tonight. I'm so tired.'

Naturally Jenny couldn't disagree with that. She just got on with making a plate of sandwiches for William, so that he could go into the sitting room and join his brother and grandfather setting up the train set.

'Hey!' exclaimed Jenny as Alexander grabbed one of the sandwiches she'd made for William. 'These are not for you.'

Alexander grinned as he chewed the sandwich.

'Make a few more, Sunshine. I expect the railway builders will want some before they retire.'

Jenny made a face at him, but she wasn't really cross, just pleased to think her efforts were appreciated.

'You don't mind me calling you Sunshine, do you? It's just a nickname. You have brought sunshine back into my life.'

'Not for long!' she warned him, and was sorry when his face lost its smile.

But it was the truth. Her stay had been prolonged, but would end soon. She would return home, and start looking for a ground floor flat. She would be sorry to leave his mother's home and had no idea where she would go.

He was avoiding looking at her as he filled the dishwasher. She wondered what was going on in his mind.

'I wonder what has happened to Belle,' she said, suddenly thinking of the cat. 'I suppose she took fright when the fire started. I do hope she is all right.'

Alexander looked down at the kitchen floor, towards the cat bed and bowls area, then checked to see if the cat flap was still working.

He remarked, 'Cats can go off for days. Just leave some food and water out for her. She'll be back when things quieten down.'

When I'm gone, thought Jenny, with a pang of regret. But she shrugged. Life had to go on; neither she and Alexander were prepared to say exactly what they thought their future should be.

More mundane things had to be sorted; for example, they needed to get more food in. She asked him to make out a list.

William's voice sounded downstairs and Alexander said he hoped he wouldn't spoil the fun going on in the sitting room.

'We could go and join them,' suggested Jenny. 'I'll get a tray of nibbles ready. Joan made some jam tarts — '

'Joan?' Alexander's head jerked round to face her with a puzzled look.

Jenny began to fill some bowls with crisps and nuts and took the jam tarts out of the cupboard where Joan had put them.

Jenny laughed to see the amazed look Alexander gave her. 'Has she been here?'

'If you mean Polly's mother,' said Jenny calmly laying the tarts out on a plate, 'yes, she came to protest about me spending the night with you.'

'The witch!'

'No, no, Alexander.' Jenny calmly licked her finger that had a dab of jam on it. 'You mustn't say that. Joan is understandably distraught at losing Polly — as you are. She went into your room and saw me asleep on your bed. So, she presumed you and I had spent the night together.'

Alexander saw her smile and broke into a laugh.

'I had the cleaning lady to contend with too — both very acid-looking — but when Joan called William a hooligan and refused to get him breakfast, I did get annoyed.'

'What happened?' Alexander put down the list he was writing and looked at her anxiously.

209

'Oh, I said I would get William's breakfast, which I proceeded to do, then I took his meal up him and told him to tidy his room as Rosie wanted to clean it. He didn't like that but ate his breakfast while I set up his smart phone for him. When I got back into the kitchen Rosie had begun her cleaning and Joan broke down in tears.'

'Poor Joan!' Alexander said sympathetically.

Jenny was pleased to hear him show compassion. He had suffered from Polly's death and he appreciated Polly's mother would too.

'Then, Joan offered to make the jam tarts.'

'Let's go and enjoy them, then,' he said, offering to carry the tray loaded with snacks.

'One other thing,' Jenny said. 'You'll be pleased to hear that William and his grandmother are now friends.'

Alexander almost dropped the heavy tray.

'How did you perform that miracle?'

'I didn't!'

'How did it happen then?'

'William noticed the fire from his bedroom window. He sensibly rang the fire brigade and came downstairs to warn us, saying that it was his fault he hadn't made sure the fire was out when you'd told him to. He was sobbing his heart out, poor lad, because he loves you and hated to think he had caused your shed and tools to be destroyed. And Joan put her arms around him.'

Alexander was visibly moved to hear all this. It confirmed in her mind that he had been worried about Joan's attitude and it was a relief for him to hear that the antagonism between the two of them was now over.

Jenny said simply, 'Let's get going.'

In the sitting room Cyril was sitting on the carpet supervising the model railway, which he was enjoying, but on seeing Jenny and Alexander entering the room, he called for help to get up.

Alexander fetched him a brandy from

the drinks cabinet saying, 'You deserve this,' and Cyril took it eagerly.

Everyone enjoyed the food as the little engine rattled round the railway tracks, and Toby was in his element being in charge of the controls. William, too, was only having minor quarrels with his brother about what the engine should do next and was delighted to have more tasty things to nibble for his supper.

Cyril was helped to sit on the sofa beside Jenny and, having eaten, said to her, 'Miss Warner — '

'Jenny.'

'Thank you, Jenny for the food.'

'It's a pleasure.'

Cyril shifted his feet and said quietly, 'Jenny — this Hornby set was new and Toby told me you bought it for him.'

Jenny, who had a mouthful, swallowed and nodded.

Cyril continued, 'And William showed me his new smartphone he said you gave him.'

'Yep.'

'And Katie is so proud of her necklace.'

Jenny said nothing.

'It made me wonder, as I know your car that William smashed was a top of the range model, how Alexander is going to replace it.'

Jenny put down her plate and brushed the crumbs off her lap. All the family were talking together. She turned to Cyril and whispered, 'Well, the car will be covered by my insurance — but can you keep a secret?'

He smiled. 'I was a captain in the Navy.'

Jenny smiled back. 'Well then, if you promise not to tell the children . . . I am a millionaire. I won the Lottery a couple of years ago.'

'Ah,' said Cyril. 'That explains everything.'

'It's not that simple, Cyril. Money does not buy everything — it creates problems.'

He pressed his lips together. 'Alexander?'

Jenny blushed. She continued talking softly.

'Alexander and I like each other very much, but we are not lovers. We met because I have a flat in his mother's house in London. I intend to make my own life.'

'The high seas are not the place for someone like you. You need a safe harbour.'

'I do. But I have not been asked to stay here.'

Cyril took a sip of his drink.

'He is embarrassed by your wealth.'

Jenny looked over at the man she was growing to love and gave a sigh.

'It's too soon after Polly's death,' she said.

Cyril smiled ruefully. 'Having been in the Navy, I've experienced many sailors' woes. Often I had to tell them or their parents about the death of a loved one. It is something one has to get over. Losing Polly was a terrible blow to Joan and me. But our grandchildren need help, and you seem to be the person they need right now.'

'Don't think I haven't thought of that!'

Cyril patted her hand.

'Just to let you know that neither Joan or I would be upset if you did decide to berth here.'

Cyril received a warm smile from Jenny.

'Thank you.' It was all she felt she could say.

The chimes of the clock in the hall reminded everyone that the evening was progressing and some young folk needed to get to bed.

As the children were sent upstairs and Cyril helped Alexander put up the camp bed in the sitting room, Jenny went to fetch some bedlinen. The children gradually ceased their chatter and, clambering into bed, were soon happily asleep.

After Cyril had gone too, Jenny said, 'I'll sleep down here. You go to your own bed.'

'Jenny, I'm so exhausted, I could

sleep anywhere. You go upstairs, Sunshine.'

He looked all in and she didn't want to argue.

Jenny didn't take long to fall asleep either.

So much had happened that day. But nothing was solved as far as she was concerned. People may talk about Alexander and herself — may wonder about their relationship — but in the end it must depend on them.

What they wanted and what they decided to do.

12

Next morning Jenny felt peeved she had no fresh clothes to wear. She needed to get back to her flat for that reason. It was all very well wearing some of Polly's underclothes, but she didn't feel it was right to put on her outer garments. Even if some fitted her — which she doubted.

She was not annoyed to have spent several days with the family; it had been necessary with all the things that had happened.

Noticing a cup of cold tea at the side of the bed, she guessed Alexander had brought it up for her but had left it as she had been asleep. He was such a kind, thoughtful man!

Having showered and made herself look as presentable as she could, Jenny went down to the kitchen thinking the house was rather quiet.

217

Alexander was seated with his mobile to his ear. He smiled and gave her a little wave before quickly finishing his conversation.

'Good morning, Jenny! Sorry I can't make you a cooked breakfast. We're out of bacon and eggs.'

Of course — he had made a list but she hadn't got round to sending off the supermarket order.

'Where are the children?' she asked him.

'They had toast and cereal before they went off to school. They join what is called a Walking Train, calling in to collect children along the route, making them walk to school in an orderly line along the very narrow and winding country lanes — as cars frequently come along them too fast.'

Jenny thought that was a brilliant idea.

Alexander continued as he rose to put on the kettle, 'William is still asleep and I thought it best to leave him in bed this morning — he had a rough day yesterday and still has a broken arm to heal.'

He made some tea as Jenny helped herself to the remains of a packet of cereal.

'I need to get in some coffee too,' he remarked apologetically.

She wondered if he'd had any breakfast — she was discovering he never put himself first. He was instinctively unselfish and preferred to go without if there wasn't enough food to go around.

Alexander said, 'My boss has given me the day off and when we have been to the garage to select a new car for you, I can go grocery shopping.'

Jenny almost protested, *I don't need a car!* But on reflection she knew she would need one. She said she would appreciate having Alexander's help in choosing one.

'I'll just pop up and tell William we are going out. And I'll ask him to feed the cat when she comes in. I brought back tons of schoolwork for him to do.'

'Poor William!'

'Not at all, Jenny. William is a natural scholar. He'll love sorting that lot out.'

After Jenny had fetched her handbag, they went out to Alexander's old car and she grimaced.

'It is you who need a new car. Yours is a disgrace. It badly needs valeting — a deep clean.'

'I have that in mind.'

Jenny knew her priorities were not his. She shut up, thinking he didn't need any more criticism. He needed to be told what a wonderful man he was. How he was coping so well, and how everyone — including herself — thought highly of him. Going into town in a smelly, ramshackle car wasn't his choice; he must be embarrassed.

They arrived at the garage where a salesman was waiting for them.

'There are two superb sports cars which arrived yesterday that I can show you.' The salesman's smile widened as he opened the car door for Jenny. 'Would you like to follow me, madam?'

She smiled back because she already knew what she was going to buy.

After Alexander had shown his appreciation of the two models he asked Jenny, 'Have you decided which one you are going to have?'

'Oh, yes!'

'Well, I'll leave you to settle the paperwork. I'm going over to the restaurant for an all-day breakfast. What shall I order for you, Jenny?'

'The same, please.'

★ ★ ★

Some time later Jenny joined Alexander and they munched their way through two enormous platefuls of fried food. Finally Alexander sat back and sighed contentedly.

'Now we must head for the super-market,' he said.

'I'm just popping to the loo. See you outside,' Jenny said, handing him the car keys.

She wasn't surprised to see him a few

minutes later wandering up and down the car park with a puzzled expression on his face.

'I can't see your car,' he said, swiping his hair from his forehead. 'Which did you choose?'

'It's over there,' Jenny said pointing and walking towards a brand new four-by-four.

He stood gaping at her.

'That's not the kind of car you need.'

'I know that! Although I do want a small hatchback — I've ordered one. This one is for you.'

The realisation of what she'd done hit him hard. He looked at her angrily.

'Where's my car?' he shouted, making other customers turn to look at them.

'Your old banger was given in part payment — it's probably on the way to the dump.'

'I have some of my things in it.'

'Yes. They have been put in your new car.'

He stamped up and down, swearing,

she had no doubt. 'I can't afford a new car,' she heard him grumble. 'Certainly not a top-of-the-range one like this. I'll be in debt forever.'

'Go and get the groceries, then take me home,' snapped Jenny. 'And don't forget cat food.'

He had no choice but to get into his new car. Jenny noticed how reverently his hands stroked the upholstery, and he examined the controls as though he was already half-familiar with them without having to consult the manual.

Having accepted he had no choice, Alexander seemed to be enjoying driving the Range Rover. He just couldn't seem to believe he was sailing through the traffic in a car he'd obviously always wanted.

Glancing at him, Jenny noticed the little smile on his lips. She was sure she'd chosen the right car for him. It was spacious for his family, sturdy enough to cope with countryside conditions and suitable for running up high mileage, as he needed to do as a surveyor looking at properties.

Most of all, despite his annoyance he liked it!

Jenny relished the smell of the new vehicle's interior, so much better than the awful stench in his old car. Whether her bold action was the right one, she was not sure. Alexander might never forgive her.

Maybe, if he had been considering her as his second wife, he would think he'd never be able to trust her because of her impulsive behaviour. It might cause all kinds of trouble in the future.

Then she had to face the fact that he was angry. Mad that she'd gone behind his back to swap the car he thought *she* was going to get for one she wanted to get for *him*.

She, of course, had no desire for a sports car. A little runaround was all she wanted and needed. And she'd ordered one.

In the meantime, Alexander was taking her back to her flat as she'd told him to do.

Was this to be the end of their friendship? Would he just dump her there and say goodbye?

Would he insist on trying to pay her back for two cars — the sporty model William had wrecked, and his new Range Rover? He was well aware he need not, as she could easily afford both cars. It was the humiliation he felt, perhaps, that was the trouble.

They didn't speak.

She was convinced her generosity was not misplaced. He was obviously thinking it was. Hadn't he told her not to give him, or his family, any more presents? And look what she'd done!

Oh well, she tried to comfort herself. If he was so touchy about her having money, then perhaps hoping to marry him would be a mistake.

On arriving at Mrs Sharman's house, they noticed a taxi outside the front door.

Alexander craned his neck. 'I wonder what's up. Is my mother going out for an appointment?'

Jenny noticed a pile of suitcases by the front door and frowned. She had hoped to get Mrs Sharman alone for a chat — to explain her side of the story about what had happened to her in the past few days.

She slid out of the passenger seat before Alexander had time to walk around the big vehicle and let her out.

He strode to the front door and charged in without ringing the bell — well, it was his mother's home after all.

Jenny had difficulty opening the boot of the new car, but finally managed to extract her small case and, with her handbag slung over her shoulder, began to climb the steps. Then she almost fell backwards — because there in the doorway stood her father!

'Dad!'

Almost in tears, she stumbled up the steps to rush into his arms.

'There, there,' he said stroking her hair and kissing her wet cheek. 'I'm sorry to have given you a shock. I should have warned you that I was arriving today but my flight was earlier than I thought. I've finally done it — taken early retirement.'

'Dad, I'm so . . . so very pleased to see you.'

Indeed she was. His diplomatic work had meant that he'd been away for most of her childhood, with only occasional visits home.

And now he was home for good — at the very moment when she was trying to piece her own life together, when his fatherly advice would be greatly appreciated to sort out her mixed emotions.

His arm around her shoulders, Mr Warner walked with his daughter into the hall where Mrs Sharman and her son were talking earnestly.

Alexander greeted Jenny's father pleasantly but said, 'I must get back to my home as I have groceries to put away and children due home from school shortly.'

'Wait a moment!' Jenny cried. 'Dad needs somewhere to stay. He can use my flat, and I'll go home with you. But I must go up quickly and get a few things.'

Everyone looked at each other in amazement.

Mrs Sharman said, 'I have no objection to Mr Warner staying here.' In fact she looked pleased with the idea.

Alexander flicked his hair off his forehead and looked down at his feet. His rather dirty casual shoes contrasted with her father's shiny leather lace-ups.

Jenny hesitated. She and Mrs Sharman had made up their minds about the situation; it was the men who had to decide now.

Being a diplomat, Mr Warner had the skills necessary to smooth over the atmosphere he'd detected between his daughter and the young man who'd brought her home. They chatted briefly while the women greeted each other warmly.

'Go up and get what you need, Jenny. I'll wait for you,' Alexander said as he thawed under the charm of the older man.

Jenny marvelled at how quickly and easily she could scale the stairs that until recently she could only climb slowly and painfully — but she had still firmly in her mind the idea that she'd have to look for new accommodation on one level. Her father would be looking for a new home, now that he was retiring. But at present the situation of him being in the flat was ideal both for Mrs Sharman and her father. She didn't like being in the large house alone and she could help him adjust to living in England again.

Aware that Alexander was waiting for her below, Jenny grabbed a bigger suitcase, and crammed into it clothes from her chest of drawers and wardrobe — everyday wear, some toiletries and her nightwear.

Fortunately, her kitchen was in good order and her fridge and freezer contained recently-bought food, so her father wouldn't go hungry. She didn't have time to change the sheets on her bed but put freshly laundered sheets and towels out for him. As he was used to living alone since her mother died, she felt that with Mrs Sharman downstairs to consult, he would be happy in the flat.

Alexander had guessed she'd have heavier luggage, and had come upstairs to carry it for her.

'Let me take your stuff,' he said.

He seemed in a better mood, but she could tell he still wasn't entirely happy with her. If she hadn't been obliged to go with him, she felt he would have left her in her flat quite happily.

Once downstairs and waved off by their parents, Jenny sat stiffly in the luxurious passenger seat as Alexander drove off towards Thrompton — at rather too fast a speed, she thought, but dared not mention. *Serve him right if he gets a speeding ticket*, she thought.

'Let's hope we get home before the youngsters arrive,' was his only comment.

Once again, she was pleased to see how well the car suited him. He was like a child with a new toy. She noticed him looking at the dials, switching some on and off and trying out the radio when the car was at rest at traffic lights.

'Look,' Jenny said. 'We can't arrive home not speaking — what will the children think?'

She noticed him grip the steering wheel.

'You are my guest, Jenny. I will be polite to you.'

'I should hope so!'

After a while he said, 'When is your car going to be delivered? I presume the garage will bring it to the cottage.'

'Tomorrow. Then if we are still not on speaking terms, I can move into a hotel.'

'Very funny.'

She huffed. 'You don't seem to realise it is your fault — your attitude that needs changing. We are not living in Victorian times when a woman was dependent on men for her living. If it was you with wealth, do you think I'd mind?'

'You would. Yes — you'd be thinking I was trying to take advantage of you.'

'Rubbish!'

They were coming off the motorway now and heading towards the countryside. Jenny knew she had to say something to clear the air, so she said boldly, 'Alexander, you needed a new car. You've got a new car. The kids will think you bought it. So pretend you did. What the hell does it matter who bought it? And the little car I've ordered for myself is what I really want — not a flashy sports car! It'll be a joy for me to have it to get around in. Just as this one is a joy to you — and don't say it isn't. I know it suits you. So just shut up about who paid for it. And for goodness' sake even if you can't bring yourself to thank me — at least put a smile on your face for your children's sake.'

She held her breath.

Was he about to explode with anger?

She'd put her point of view — but it was easy for her to be generous when it didn't hurt her bank balance to do so.

For Alexander it was a different matter. Not badly off, with a good job, he'd been hard hit when his wife died. He'd had extra expenses thrown at him: the funeral, extra home help, William smashing up her car. And now the fire meant he would have to pay for materials for a replacement shed and another large lawn mower, as he had an acre of grass to cut. Oh yes — not forgetting him having had to take time off work to cope with his family responsibilities. What a heap of bad luck he'd had!

Who was on his side? Who was trying to understand how he felt? How difficult it might be for his ego to have his dream car thrust at him making him feel uncomfortable to have to accept such a well-meant gift, but with such a breathtaking price tag? She could have got him a cheaper four-by-four. She just wanted to give him the best.

Because she loved him — that was why.

On top of everything, she was not helping by being judgmental. He couldn't help feeling the way he did about her generosity. It was sad in a way; she felt it meant he would never ask her to marry him.

Would he stop the car at the nearest hotel and throw her out?

She was aware of Alexander taking some deep breaths, then she heard a choking noise. Alarmed, she turned to see what was the matter with him.

He had begun to laugh.

'Sunshine,' he spluttered. 'You're right! I did need a new car. You have the money to spend how you like. The trifling expense of a top spec Range Rover shouldn't bother either of us.'

They both giggled helplessly all the way back to the cottage.

13

William must have heard the car on the drive and came running to open the front door.

Apparently failing to notice the shiny new four-by-four, he cried out urgently, 'You'll never guess what's happened!'

Jenny heard Alexander groan.

'I'll deal with this, Jenny. Can you put the frozen stuff in the freezer?'

He threw her the car keys, which she managed to catch, and disappeared with William into the house.

Jenny had difficulty opening the boot door, but persevered until she did. Then she located two bags of items that needed to be refrigerated. She found a cool bag tipped over, and refilled it with as much of the freezer stuff she could carry.

There was no sign of Alexander — or William — as she staggered into the house carrying the heavy bags. At least, they were heavy for her. Thank goodness her knee was no longer a problem.

Puzzled, she put them down in the hall and yelled, 'Anyone at home?'

William darted out of the kitchen and Jenny was relieved to see a wide smile on his face.

'We're all in the kitchen.' William was already turning to hurry back there.

'All? Who is here?'

'Come and see!'

So, leaving the groceries, she did.

Alexander was kneeling by the cat basket.

What she'd long suspected was coming had arrived — little balls of fluffy kittens.

Belle looked up at her with dreamy eyes and gave a long, loud meow! She was hungry, having been away for a couple of days and giving birth.

William seemed to want to be in charge, telling his father that when his brother and sister came home from school they must not disturb the cat family or make a noise. He added importantly, 'I've decided I want to be a vet when I grow up.'

Alexander winked at Jenny.

'I guess we'd better put the groceries away quietly. I'll go and get the rest of the stuff from the car. Can you feed Belle?'

William looked at her with pleading eyes.

'Jenny — I'll feed Belle. Please could you make something for tea instead — I'm starving!'

Jenny wasn't surprised as he'd been left alone in the house for hours — and the food cupboards had been bare!

'One big family meal coming up,' she replied with a smile.

Slipping off her jacket and putting on an apron, Jenny was happy to get to work cooking merrily.

Soon pans of potatoes, carrots and water ready for the runner beans were bubbling on the hob, and the frying pan made ready for hamburgers.

William opened the large box of forty pouches of cat food, selecting one and opening it. Belle abandoned her three kittens to eat, purring.

Jenny found herself humming as she stuffed some cooking apples with sultanas. Then she made some custard. She was feeling ridiculously happy to be back in her kitchen. Or at least, doing her job of feeding the family. But she realised that, even after stocking up with food, they would soon need more. Perhaps she should offer to do that job for Alexander? Would he let her?

Alexander rushed out to greet the walking train of children, who had arrived at the gate, to ask them to keep their voices down. When he explained why, of course all the youngsters wanted to come and see the newborn kittens.

Standing guard by the front door, he said he would allow them in two by two, Katie and Toby first — although Toby also wanted to know whose car was in the drive.

'It's our new car,' replied Alexander, a little uncertainly.

Toby jumped up and down in excitement.

'Wow!'

The two walking train helpers were there to keep the children in order while they took turns to peer in at Belle's offspring.

Eventually all the hushed chatter and little feet retreated, leaving the family in peace.

Belle, having finished all the food in her bowl, decided to hop outside through the cat flap, and the humans settled down to their meal.

There was a sudden clunk and they turned to see that Belle had brought in another kitten!

Jenny said, 'Let her be. Sit down, Katie, and have your pudding. The kittens won't run away.'

She stopped herself, realising that she was now ordering the family about — but she received a reassuring smile from Alexander.

Katie said, 'Dad — after tea, will you take us all out for a ride in your new car?'

William licked his lips as he finished off his baked apple and asked, 'What new car?'

'Dad's!' chorused Toby and Katie.

William was up like a shot.

'I must go and see it. What make is it?'

Alexander growled, 'Sit down! You are not to go anywhere near it unless I'm there.'

As William looked crestfallen, recalling his recent escapade, Jenny put in cheerfully, 'I'm having my new car delivered tomorrow.'

'You're not to go anywhere near Jenny's car either,' Alexander ordered, scraping the last of the custard off his bowl.

The clatter of putting away clean dishes and re-loading the dishwasher was soon over, and the children clambered eagerly into the four-by-four, exclaiming at its spaciousness.

Jenny took her place in the front seat and Alexander took them for a half-hour drive through the countryside, warning them all sternly that this car was to be kept clean and tidy at all times and any sweet wrappers were to be put in the bin at home.

★ ★ ★

Once again Alexander assured Jenny he was happy to sleep downstairs on the camp bed, and she didn't argue. She longed to sleep with him — but before that could happen, there were so many decisions to be made about their future. And when Alexander thrust at her a pile of papers about properties that he thought she might like to move into, she was soon absorbed in looking at them while he put the children to bed.

He was not presuming she wanted to marry him. And the tiff they had about her buying him a new car only reinforced her fear that he would never get over her superior financial status. So she had better get on with searching for a new place to live — although it gave her a cold feeling to think of having to do it.

There was one property — a bungalow — which did look very inviting. It was not far from Mrs Sharman's house and was one of three built on the land where there had been a large family house. It had no garden to speak of, just a small patio area. She put that paper aside as she thought it might suit her — or her father, for that matter.

Then there was a kind of community group of bungalows, with several homes on the site and several amenities listed where the owners of the properties could meet up if they wanted company. It certainly looked very well designed and was on the edge of a town, so that if she wished she could take a bus rather than use her car to go shopping.

Of course, it wasn't as private as she'd been used to . . . and close neighbours could be a trial if they didn't get on or she didn't want to socialise too much.

One really luxurious house had a swimming pool — and wouldn't the fabulous kitchen be wonderful to work in? Except that she would rarely have any cooking to do for anyone. Alexander's children would enjoy visiting and using the pool — but how often would that be?

And what was she going to do with all the time she'd have living alone again? How was she going to cope, when she knew in her heart that she loved Alexander?

'Hello Sunshine! Have you decided which ones you'd like to visit?' Alexander's voice penetrated her thoughts.

Her smile at him was a little watery.

'Yes, I have three I've picked out.'

'Right. Good. As showing properties is part of my job, I won't have to go into London tomorrow. As soon as we've seen the little ones off to school, we can go and see the properties you've selected.'

'What about my new car?'

'You can ring the garage and ask them to deliver it later in the day.'

★   ★   ★

Jenny was restless that night. She wanted Alexander in bed beside her, not downstairs on the camp bed — not that he ever complained.

Perhaps he didn't feel the same way about her — was a housekeeper all he wanted?

She got up early and decided to get herself a cup of tea. Putting on her slippers and dressing gown and pulling a comb through her hair, she crept down to the kitchen, switched on one light and then noticed Belle was in her basket.

She went to stroke her, hoping the Siamese wouldn't start meowing loudly as they can do.

It was then she noticed there were five kittens!

'Oh, Belle! Don't bring us any more!'

Alexander would have to find homes for them — another burden on him. And he must take the cat to the vet, to make sure she didn't have any more in the future. The kits weren't pedigree Siamese to sell — they were just adorable little moggies needing good homes in a few weeks' time.

Just as *she* needed a new home.

Or did she? Wasn't this cosy home, right here, where she wanted to stay?

Feeding the cat and putting the kettle on to make tea, she wondered if she should take a cup to Alexander. He'd often brought one for her, hadn't he?

So she made a pot of tea and carried it along the corridor. She stood outside the sitting room door, wondering whether she should knock before going in.

Suddenly the door swung open and there he stood, a magnificent sight of male physical perfection in his underpants. His eyes were bleary with sleep, his hair like a haystack in the wind.

What it would be like to be held against that wide muscled chest with those strong arms she couldn't help wondering!

Stunned at her reaction, it was a wonder Jenny didn't drop the teacup. Alexander was quick-witted enough to put out his hand and grasp it.

'Is this for me?' he asked in a surprised voice, trying to flick back the mop of hair that always seemed to fall over his eyes. He needed another haircut — but she understood why he just hadn't had time to phone and arrange it.

'Yes, it is — Belle has had her breakfast and her five kittens are at the milk bar now.'

He blinked. 'Did I hear you say five kittens?'

'Yes. Last time I looked in her basket there were five.'

He winced and took a slurp of tea.

'Don't worry. I'm sure we'll find a home for them all — and it won't be necessary for a few weeks yet.'

She hoped he hadn't noticed her saying *we*, because she didn't intend to be around in a few weeks' time. But he didn't appear to notice and said, 'I must get the kids up for school.'

A glance at the hall clock showed that it was indeed time to get going.

'You go upstairs and have a shower in your own bedroom,' she instructed. 'I'll start getting the breakfast ready for when you all come down.'

After he'd scooted upstairs, she made herself busy in the kitchen.

★ ★ ★

Alexander had put on a smart suit, silk tie and polished shoes, as he did whenever he was taking a client around to see properties. He even adopted his salesman's patter as they got into his Range Rover and discussed the places they were going to see that day.

She had decided to wear a pretty floral dress and jacket as the weather was decidedly autumnal. Looking chic, but not too dressed-up, she thought it would be appropriate with him wearing a business suit. Her leather cross-body handbag matched her heeled shoes.

'You look terrific.' Alexander smiled approvingly.

'So do you — well, except for your hair.' She spoke candidly.

He brushed his hair away from his forehead with a quick swipe, but it fell back immediately.

'I promise to get it cut as soon as I can,' he retorted, which made her think contritely that she shouldn't criticise him — he had enough coming from Polly's mum, and his three children.

Alexander never seemed to want to defend himself. Not at all like his surgeon brother Jim — no one would dare criticise him — or if they did, the surgeon would glare disdainfully at them!

Jenny determined to try and be supportive, although today was going to be difficult as she hadn't the slightest notion of what kind of property she was looking for.

'What you have to decide on is where you really want to live,' Alexander said. 'Are you looking for a town house or something more rural?'

'Er . . . ' Jenny found it difficult to reply.

'Let's look at the town one first, shall we?'

'OK.'

It was in the direction of where his mother's house was, one of three bungalows built on the site of an old house that had been pulled down.

'The bungalows are quite separate, Jenny. With the landscaped gardens, you can pay for a gardener and then you don't have to worry if you don't want to do any yourself.'

It was all too neat and tidy. Tiny, manicured lawns made Jenny feel she shouldn't step on the grass. In the flower beds there wasn't a weed in sight. There was a private patio with a few carefully laid-out pots, rather like a continental out-of-door picnic area. But who would she entertain?

The inside of the bungalow was well designed for a person like herself. Alexander waved her through each room and opened cupboards to show her the ample storage space.

'It is brand new — you'll be able to decorate the rooms and furnish it to suit yourself. And you are detached, well insulated from hearing anyone's TV or other noises neighbours make.'

'That's a point,' Jenny said, not enthusiastic about living so isolatedly. Nor, for that matter, about being in such a pristine property.

It may suit some, she thought, *but for me I'd feel restricted. Like having to be on my best behaviour all the time, afraid to make a mess anywhere. It was different somehow in my flat.*

'There's a bus stop outside on a route that runs straight into Victoria, the central bus station. So you can go shopping or go to the theatre in the West End whenever you like, if you don't want to drive in.'

What would I want to shop for?

Jenny wouldn't need much for day-to-day living. She'd order anything she wanted online — wouldn't she?

Noticing her lack of enthusiasm, Alexander said, 'Shall we go and see the next property?'

She nodded.

The next place was in some ways just the opposite, in that the property for sale was one of a cosy group of houses. They were part of an old coaching inn that had been renovated. What were once the outbuildings — the stables, the bakery and the laundry — had all been rebuilt to make private residences of character.

'Delightful,' commented Jenny, as she really thought they were. 'But not for me.'

Alexander sounded a bit miffed. 'Why not?'

'Neighbours too close.'

He sighed. 'You elected to look at it.'

'Sorry,' she said in a small voice.

Jenny was contrite, as they had driven miles to reach this property. Having got here, he was understandably annoyed that she didn't even want to get out of the car and examine it.

'Let's go and have a bite to eat before I take you to see the last property.'

Going along the road, they chose a quiet wayside restaurant that gave them the chance to relax and talk about other things. Jenny was keen to learn what Alexander liked and wanted because as long as she'd known him, all he seemed to want to do was to please his family.

They discovered they both enjoyed travel, and discussed holiday destinations they would like to visit. They enjoyed the same kind of TV programmes, as well as walks in the countryside.

'I like cooking too,' said Jenny, who was enjoying her ploughman's lunch.

'I know you do. You're extremely good at it.'

'And I think I'd enjoy doing a little gardening. A plot can quickly get overgrown.' She was thinking of Polly's abandoned garden. 'But I'd have to learn something about tending gardens.'

He might have been thinking of Polly's abandoned garden too, as his face suddenly looked a little strained. Quickly she said, 'They have given me too many pickled onions and too much cheese — would you like them?'

Alexander didn't object to helping himself to what he wanted from her plate. Then he sat back to enjoy the non-alcoholic beer while Jenny indulged in a bowl of fruit crumble and custard.

Scratching his eyebrow, he said, 'Well — I suppose we'd better get going and take a look at this last property. It's on the way home, and very different from the ones you've seen so far.'

Jenny went to the ladies, hoping this property they were going to see was going to be more suitable for her.

Washing her hands, she looked at herself in the mirror.

At twenty-nine, she still looked remarkably young for her age. Her blue eyes and curly brown hair were her best features — as well as her sunny smile. No one would call her a beautiful woman — although they might say she had a healthy complexion. And she had a good figure, too.

She'd been tied up with Marvin for far too long while all her friends had married, and when she decided not to marry him she'd taken a while to get into a frame of mind in which she could reconsider any new attachment. Then, crash! Money had come and swamped her.

Now she'd come to terms with her situation, she must decide what she wanted out of life.

Yes, she did like Alexander, and his family. That she was certain of. But what did he feel about her? That she was much less sure about.

If she liked this property they were about to go and see, which he said was on the way home, did she want to be living so near him? Wouldn't it be better to go abroad, live somewhere far away?

If he did want to marry her, how were they to get over his discomfort with her financial situation? And the fact that he was ten years older than her? Not to mention his children. He may feel she would not want to mother them.

And did she want children of her own?

These questions had to be answered. She couldn't have him wasting time trying to find her a place when she had no idea what she wanted.

What was really needed was for them to discuss the rift between them, and be willing to compromise — or part.

14

'This property is unique,' Alexander informed her unnecessarily. It certainly seemed to Jenny to be ultra-modern as she gazed out of the car window at the sprawling low-level building. It was luxurious-looking though, in its woodland setting.

'It looks like a hospital or something,' she commented. Then she wished she hadn't, as it would seem as though she had already decided she didn't like it.

'Wait until you see the inside.' Alexander slipped out of the car and went around to open the passenger seat door for her.

'Well, I suppose it won't hurt to look,' Jenny said, and again regretted that remark. She could see by the look on his face that he was annoyed she'd shown no enthusiasm.

'It's a woodland setting. Only been

up a few years. The architect is world-famous.'

'Why is it up for sale?'

'I understand the people who had it built decided to emigrate.'

She felt tempted to say, *I'm not surprised*, but held her tongue. Some people liked modern architecture and she had no quarrel with that. Only she wasn't that keen on the design of some. Her thoughts switched to a cottage-type house, old brickwork and small windows — with perhaps a modern addition of a new kitchen and . . . just like Alexander's house, in fact!

'You wouldn't be alone here. The caretaker cum gardener has a house nearby.'

That didn't thrill Jenny. Perhaps she wouldn't like the caretaker — or his wife and kids?

Maybe he wouldn't like her working on the garden, especially as she knew so little about it.

Jenny stood looking at the grand

entrance and expanse of hall beyond. The rooms would be large and she wouldn't want to have to clean them — she would require a cleaner. The large windows would take a a full day to polish, she reckoned.

Nothing homely about it at all.

'It's impressive,' Alexander said, trying to sound as though he liked it, 'quite palatial.'

She didn't want to impress anyone.

'I was thinking of finding a home — not a palace!' she blurted out.

He slapped one of the clipped shrubs that lined the path that led up to the entrance with the papers he was carrying.

'Well, you might as well see inside while you're here. You might change your mind.'

No way, she thought, but she could see he wanted to go inside as he'd taken the keys from his pocket so she let him show her inside.

Jenny could tell he was annoyed. She couldn't blame him. After all, she'd selected the properties and told him she wanted to see them. He was merely doing what she'd asked him to do.

And was it surprising that he seemed to be regretting taking the day to show her places when she was so unappreciative?

But what was the use of trying to appear enthusiastic when her true feelings did not allow her to like the places he'd been showing her?

She'd asked him to find her a place to live. It was her fault that he was becoming angry with her, even though all she was doing was making it clear to him that she wasn't in the slightest bit interested in what he was trying to sell her.

But what could she do about the situation?

At least she should let him escort her through the house and try and show some interest in it.

So they began viewing the house as an estate agent would take his client around.

The reception rooms were large, suitable for a family and entertaining. The bedrooms were fitted out with the finest modern features, including ensuites.

Electrical fittings were all over the place as were lights, and as the afternoon had turned gloomy, the various lamps Alexander switched on were cheering.

'You could have a TV in each bedroom,' he commented.

She stopped herself from retorting that she didn't see a need for that. Or four bedrooms, either — although one could be an office and another a sewing room, she supposed.

It was possible that her father might like to come and live here with her.

The kitchen she did like — it was stylish and functional. But Jenny reckoned it would be tiring traipsing about the large area when cooking. Especially when she was only preparing her own meals.

'What do you think of it?'

She became aware of Alexander's question.

'Very nice.'

He looked at her quizzically.

She thought she'd better say something more positive.

'I like the Aga cooker; its warmth makes a kitchen cosy.'

Of course, it wasn't lit at the moment as the house was empty.

'Lots of cupboards in here,' remarked Alexander, opening some to show her.

Jenny was aware that some women had difficulty with storage in a kitchen, but she was going to be on her own, wasn't she? Did she need to fill the kitchen cupboards with every spice and kitchen aid? No, they wouldn't stay in-date, and she always preferred to buy fresh ingredients before she began cooking.

She wandered about looking here and there, admiring some things, and keeping quiet about anything she would change if she moved in.

'Now I must show you the outstanding feature of this house,' said Alexander, opening the door and indicating the way they should walk.

And when they got there, it most certainly did impress her. When he opened the double glass doors at the end of a corridor Jenny could smell the chlorine aroma of a swimming pool. Yes, it was a private pool!

'Oooh!' she gasped. Even if she wasn't a keen swimmer, having a luxury pool and hot tub like this was magical to see.

My, what a gorgeous sight! The soft lighting showed a pool filled with inviting blue tiles that coloured the water. Decorative features around it included Greek-style pillars and tiled murals. Sun beds and easy chairs were grouped near the patio windows that looked out over the landscaped court-yard gardens outside.

For a few moments Jenny stood and blinked.

She could imagine white-jacketed

waiters with trays of drinks moving around serving the guests at a pool party, chattering guests and background music, as well as the laughter of children enjoying the water.

Mesmerised, she walked further into the area noting the changing rooms tastefully situated alongside the pool, heading for the patio doors, so that she could look outside.

Walking beside the pool, she suddenly found her shoe skidding along the floor.

'Ahh! Oooooh! Help!'

Her sudden scream echoed around the pool as she found herself sliding towards the deep water. Frightened to lose her balance, Jenny put out her hands for something to grasp. Something to hold onto and regain her balance — but there was nothing.

'Oooh! No!' she yelled, slipping even faster forward as the tiles near the water sloped downwards, designed to keep the water in the pool.

Screaming again in terror, she saw in

front of her the lapping, deep blue water — and nothing to prevent her sliding in. With an enormous splash she slid into the deep end of the swimming pool!

The impact made her scream again. The water in the pool was not heated, and the chill of it took her breath away.

Jenny couldn't swim well at the best of times. Being suddenly out of control and finding herself sinking into deep water petrified her. Taken unawares, she didn't have time to close her eyes and she saw bubbles surrounding her. Down under the water she went. Then she bobbed up, struggling and gulping water. She thought her end had come.

Thrashing her arms and legs she clumsily trod water, crying and screaming in between gulps of water.

Alexander had whipped off his jacket and shoes and neatly dived into the pool to rescue her. The waves he created splashed over her and sent ripples against her face, so that she couldn't see as she struggled not to drown.

Suddenly she felt him cup her head firmly in his hands and hold it above the water as he shouted, 'I've got you.' He took a gulp of air and added calmly, 'Just relax, Jenny, I'm going to pull you out of the water.'

With the skill of a life-saver, Alexander then lay on his back and pulled her on top of him. Although she was still choking, and frightened out of her wits, he was able to float her towards the swimming pool steps using his powerful legs to swim backstroke.

Crying, gulping and shivering with fright Jenny clung to the ladder steps he had brought her to.

'Just stay there a minute. Hold onto the steps and get your breath. I'll help you out of the water in a minute.'

Leaving her clinging like a leech to the handrail of the steps, he left her and swam a little further away. Then he put his hands on the side of the pool and raised himself enough to bring one of his legs up and ease his body out of the water.

Having got out, he turned to crouch down by the ladder steps and said, 'Give me your hand Jenny. Now step up carefully — no hurry, take your time. I've got hold of you.'

Dripping wet, with their clothes clinging to their bodies, they were soon standing on the walkway outside the pool, shivering, Jenny holding onto Alexander for support.

'Sorry about that,' he said, as though her near-drowning experience was no more than him splashing her with his car wheels going through a puddle.

Jenny was in no mood to accept apologies. Still, if he hadn't been there, she wouldn't have got out of the water at all!

Chattering teeth prevented her from saying anything anyway. All she could think of was that she was very wet and cold. And all she wanted to do was to put her arms around him and press herself up to his warmth.

He used his finger to wipe her dripping hair off her face and then vigorously rubbed her back.

His own hair hung down his face while rivulets ran down his shoulders and back. The crisp white shirt he'd put on that morning was plastered to his wide chest as though he was naked.

Her awareness gradually shifted from her shock and discomfort to appreciating him having his arms snugly around her.

He held her just as he'd held her on the day of the fire — just as she'd comforted him after the tragedy of losing his shed and gardening equipment, but this time he was comforting her.

After several minutes they began to realise they were in a dilemma. They were shivering in their soaking clothes. They had no towels to dry off, or dry clothes to put on.

Realising Jenny was still unsteady and shaking, Alexander, with his arms supporting her, walked her to one of the pool recliner chairs and sat her down. Then he walked bck to pick up his dry jacket, which he put around her shoulders.

'There,' he said, 'That should warm you up.'

It did — a bit.

She looked up into his concerned eyes.

'Why did I slip?' she asked.

'I reckon someone has been using the pool and after their swim, washing their hair with a very slimy shampoo, which they carelessly didn't hose down properly before they left. So, the tiled floor by one changing cubicle was very slippery.'

For some reason, Jenny began to giggle and feeling her quaking with mirth against him, Alexander began to laugh too.

'Oh dear, oh dear! Now what shall we do?'

They could see the funny side of their predicament.

But Jenny knew something else too.

She knew with every fibre of her being that she loved Alexander! He had shown his care for her, diving in to get her out of the water and hugging her now to try and warm her up.

'Well — we can't stay here,' he said, still chuckling. 'I think I'd better go and see if the caretaker is in.'

'Don't do that — let's just go home,' begged Jenny. 'I don't want to be left here by myself.' She would lose her only source of warmth too.

'The caretaker might be able to assist us . . .'

'No,' she said, shaking her wet hair so that it flicked over his face. 'Even if he's in, he's unlikely to be able to help us with dry clothes, is he?'

It was certainly a good excuse for a cuddle. Cold and wet outside, their hearts were warm and at peace. He bent his head towards her and rapturously she responded.

After a quick, soft kiss, and then another longer one, Alexander said huskily, 'We can't stay here like this forever.'

Jenny's teeth chattered as she replied, 'No, we can't. We'll die of hypothermia.'

'Right.' Alexander began to loosen his hold on her. 'If you don't want me to find the caretaker — '

'He may not be in!'

'True. I made no arrangement to meet him today as I wanted to show you around the house myself. But we should get back to the car as quickly as possible — at least it has a heater in the car. Although it'll be a cold ride home in our wet things.'

'And a hot bath at the end of it,' Jenny said, realising her shoes were probably at the bottom of the swimming pool as she hadn't any on. Her handbag was bobbing about on the surface, but she hadn't the heart to ask him to dive in and retrieve it.

With Alexander's jacket wrapped around her she was ushered out of the building and the sharp breeze outside made her gasp.

Fortunately the Range Rover, designed

for rugged farm use, had a robust interior designed not to be ruined by two dripping wet passengers.

It wasn't a comfortable ride. Even with the car heater full blast and the fan on, the windows kept steaming up. Alexander dared not drive fast.

It was a ridiculous situation that shouldn't have happened. But it had. And neither of them seemed to want to moan about it . . . they were laughing on and off for most of the way back to Thrompton.

'I don't suppose you will take that place now,' Alexander said, and they burst into laughter again.

'No, I don't think I will.' She longed to say, *your cottage will suit me fine* — but even though he had told her how he appreciated the care she had given his family, and today had given her renewed hope that he was attracted to her, he hadn't asked her to live with him. Their relationship was as ambiguous as ever.

'Would madam rather I took you to a

hotel now?' he asked.

'No,' she said firmly, imagining what the receptionist at the motel would think of them arriving so bedraggled — and with no luggage. 'I want to go home.'

'Home, meaning to my house?'

'Yep.' She sneezed.

He said nothing for a while, then murmured, 'You will always be welcome there, Jenny.'

Eventually they arrived and Jenny saw her new car parked outside — the small, light grey hatchback she'd chosen. It thrilled her to see it. Alexander must have seen it too, but he was just anxious to get inside and didn't even seem to notice it.

Walking to the front door across the gravel in her stocking feet wasn't pleasant. William heard them and came to the door. He seemed glad to see them, and thought it very funny when they told him what had happened.

After a soothing, hot shower, and with dry clothes on, Jenny felt much better. Until it struck her that she'd lost her handbag — her cards, her cash, cheque book and keys!

She was effectively penniless!

15

Downstairs Jenny could hear the sound of children's voices, and she knew the walking train had arrived to drop off Katie and Toby — and to see the kittens. Hurriedly she dragged a brush through her hair, ready to face the mob.

But she needn't have worried, as she wasn't needed. William guarded the cat's basket and made sure the kits were being handled gently.

As there was no sign of Alexander, Jenny began to prepare the supper. Having plenty of groceries in, it wasn't a problem to find ingredients for a nourishing meal for the family.

'It's nice to have you here,' said Katie, smiling. 'It means we haven't got to go down and stay with Granny Davies until Dad comes and fetches us from their cottage.'

Jenny could appreciate her point of

view. And she felt pleased to be valued.

Toby was soon playing with his train set and had to be called several times to come to the table. Jenny felt she'd scored another success, giving the little boy a present of enduring interest.

There was no time to think about her missing personal items — she didn't need anything immediately, and she was too busy.

Alexander apologised for coming late to the meal. He'd had to make some phone calls.

'Uncle Jim says you may go back to school tomorrow,' he told William. 'I explained to the headmaster that you would have your arm in a sling for a couple more days, and he said that was no problem, and you are not to worry if you haven't finished all the schoolwork you were set.'

'Of course I've finished it!' William said scornfully.

Alexander winked at Jenny as if to say, *I told you he was a bright lad.* William was also becoming, like his surgeon Uncle Jim, a forthright but caring person. He'd taken charge of Belle and her kittens, and had already managed to find homes for two of them. The walking train mums had heard all about the unexpected litter, and William had persuaded a couple of them to offer to take a Siamese cross moggy.

Jenny didn't mention to Alexander that she would be staying the night again. She felt too embarrassed to admit she couldn't go to a hotel as she hadn't the means to pay for it!

Alexander didn't mention it either. He seemed to take it for granted that she would be staying.

Feeling exhausted after her 'swim', she didn't feel like discussing the financial trouble she was in. She decided she would phone her father in the morning, and sort out the problem with his help.

She was too tired to do more than clean the kitchen, make sure the kids were tucked up in bed and Alexander was in the sitting room with his camp bed ready.

'Good night!' she called out before she went upstairs.

He didn't reply. She supposed he was already asleep, and was tempted to open the sitting room door to take a look, but feared she might not succeed in resisting a goodnight kiss and be tempted to entice him upstairs with her.

★   ★   ★

Jenny's first thoughts in the morning were nothing short of a panic attack — the bedside clock showed it was nine o'clock! She had a list of urgent things she should have been up early to get on with.

After scrambling into her clothes, and brushing her hair, Jenny opened the bedroom door but heard no one about.

Of course! There wouldn't be. Alexander would be in London, taking

William to school. The young children would be walking through the winding Devon lanes on the way to school — no, they would already be in their classrooms.

Rosie, the cleaner, was due to arrive at any minute.

She wanted to try out her new car — but she couldn't, could she? The keys were probably at the bottom of the swimming pool.

But there she was wrong. On the kitchen table lay a plastic bag that looked as though it contained something soggy.

Peering at it, she recognised her wet handbag. Obviously Alexander had got up very early, motored over to the luxury bungalow, used his key to retrieve her bag from the pool, brought it back and slung it on the kitchen table for her — then driven William into London, and after that she presumed he went to his office.

All while she was snoring her head off!

What a caring, thoughtful man Alexander was. He so needed someone to care for him.

Preparing her breakfast, she noticed a letter addressed to her propped up against the toaster. She picked it up to read as Rosie let herself in, saying, 'Good morning, Miss Warner. Shall I just do my normal work?'

'Please do, Rosie. William has gone back to school today so you won't have him to deal with.'

Rosie chuckled as Jenny tore open the letter Alexander had left for her. Out fell a wad of notes that scattered over the floor.

'My goodness! No need to throw your money about,' Rosie joked, helping Jenny pick them up. 'I'll have some of these notes if you don't want them!'

'Well, some of them are for you,' said Jenny, a little embarrassed. 'Mr Sharman says in his letter that you are paid today, and you like cash.'

'That's true, I do.'

They settled the sum she was due

and Rosie went to the cleaning cupboard to collect her mop and bucket and dusters, humming merrily.

Jenny was learning afresh how important money was. Like oil in a machine, it kept the parts running smoothly.

Looking down at the fistful of notes, she found her cheeks had reddened. Embarrassment at having to use Alexander's money made her aware of how he must feel to have her spending money on him. And finally she began to understand how difficult it was for him to accept that she was a very rich woman, and he was a hardworking man who earned a good wage but had nothing like the money to spend that she had.

She signed. How could she overcome that problem?

Now that he'd retrieved her belongings, Jenny was free to spend the day as she liked. She could go for a run in her new car — provided the key still worked after its period of immersion.

She could go to the nearest bank with her soggy purse and explain what had happened. They would give her some cash and arrange for her to have new credit cards sent out.

Her confidence returned; she no longer had to think of herself with an empty wallet, needing to scrounge. Not that she'd suffered from that feeling for long. But it did recall her financial constraints before she had won the Lottery. It had reminded her of her life when she was working.

As the father of three children, Alexander would never feel well-off with so many demands on his salary. But she had no doubt that he would manage. As far as she knew, he had no expensive habits, or any ambition to live beyond his means. His young family provided him with enough satisfaction and entertainment.

A new wife might enrich his life — if he chose the right woman.

Was she that woman?

Jenny liked his young family. She'd

rarely thought about children, as she'd not come into contact with many. Some of her friends had youngsters. But Alexander's children had somehow accepted her, and she them, without any awkwardness.

If she married him, might he want her to give her fortune away, so that they were on a level footing? She didn't think that would be sensible. She considered she'd been lucky to win the Lottery. She had a right to enjoy her wealth and spend it or share it with whom she pleased. If only she knew what he thought . . .

There was a strong physical attraction between them that she could not deny. After the fire he'd held and kissed her so naturally, and she'd responded in a similar way. Then, after their dip in the swimming pool and being warmed by his hands, she was in no doubt that they had both wanted to make love.

Yes, they were physically compatible — but that was only one aspect of their relationship.

She'd told him definitely that she wanted somewhere new to live. Yesterday he had taken her at her word. But she had felt like a homing pigeon, wanting only to fly straight back to this happy, untidy extended cottage. She knew that now, and she had to face up to it.

But did he want her?

Dithering about, contemplating all the ideas that came into her head now that she was no longer in a panic about her lack of immediate funds, Jenny decided to find her car keys and take her new car out.

She explained to Rosie what she was going to do, and asked her if she would be kind enough to rinse out her still-wet clothes and put them in the dryer when she'd done the family wash. She had thought about putting some of the things in the microwave to dry them out, but decided it might be a bit risky.

'Of course I'll do that for you, Miss Warner,' Rosie said. 'It's a pleasure coming to clean in this house now you're here.'

Jenny grinned. 'I won't be too long,' she explained. 'I just want to pop into the bank and get a few things in town.'

* * *

Jenny felt odd going out with no handbag or purse — though she did have her sodden ones in the plastic bag.

Driving a new car wasn't altogether fun. She took out the manual to check on a few essential controls and then, slowly, eased the car out onto the road. As it was a weekday, the traffic was scarce and the signposts easy for her to read.

But at the car park, she found she hadn't the change for a ticket and, as she expected, her waterlogged card would not work in the machine.

Once more the feeling of being penniless struck her! She looked around and waited for someone to come so that she could ask them to change a note for her.

Fortunately, an elderly gentleman was kind enough to pay for her ticket. He wouldn't accept the ten-pound note she offered him, which embarrassed her. It also taught her that she must be careful not to embarrass others by her generosity — however well-meant.

The bank manager was busy but when she explained her predicament to the cashier, who was both amused and sympathetic, she was given a cup of coffee while the necessary paperwork was assembled to renew her cards and she was issued with a new cheque book.

Having spent so much time in the bank, she decided a quick visit to a chemist to get some essential toilet items, like a lipstick and nail file, was all she had time for. The striking of the town hall clock reminded her it was time to leave, but she stopped at a nice bakery and bought half a dozen delicious newly-baked pasties for the evening meal, as she wouldn't have time to cook from scratch when she returned to Thrompton.

She was tempted to buy cream cakes, but said a firm *no* to herself. The last thing she wanted was to anger Alexander by showering treats on the family. But she did stop at the fishmonger's for some fish tails for Belle.

Then, swinging around a corner to reach the car park, she stopped, stunned to see a pretty dress in the boutique shop window.

Walk on, walk on, she told herself.

But she pressed her nose to the window gazing at the dress, which had a matching jacket, court shoes and little handbag tastefully laid out. Quite expensive, but then why shouldn't she enjoy having some things she fancied?

Well, she couldn't resist just opening the shop door and going in.

The shop assistant was happy to see her. Jenny was the kind of customer she liked to serve.

The dress slipped over her slim shoulders and hips and looked perfect.

So did the shoes.

'The dress looks beautiful on you,' purred the assistant — but then she would flatter her if she wanted the sale. Jenny had to make up her own mind about it.

Dammit, Jenny thought. *I would like Alexander to see me in a dress occasionally as I'm always in jeans and trainers — which are fine but sometimes I just want to look feminine.*

'I'll take the lot,' she said decisively. 'Just bung them in a bag, will you? I have to be quick. My parking ticket will be running out.'

She thought the shop assistant seemed surprised that she wanted to pay by cheque, and hadn't a card. Jenny was kept waiting and tapped her foot impatiently. She had the impression that the assistant, who had popped through into the back, was phoning her bank to see if her cheque was OK.

Not that she was offended. Shops, especially small businesses, had to be careful about their transactions.

She didn't check the time as she raced towards her car — she was just thankful not to see a parking ticket fee plastered on the windscreen.

Neither did she stop to get petrol, as she noticed she had just about enough in the tank to get home. Anyway, Alexander would probably have a can of petrol at home if the tank needed topping up.

Strange how she was beginning to rely on him. But then, he looked after everyone, didn't he?

* * *

Rosie had gone by the time she arrived at the cottage, but Jenny found Joan and Cyril there.

Joan was not surprised to see her — in fact, she seemed to be waiting for her and greeted her pleasantly, saying, 'Hello Jenny, shall I make you a cup of tea?'

'Oh, yes, please. I had to dash into town to sort some things out and I haven't had breakfast.'

Joan's face broke into a smile.

'We heard you had an accident yesterday.'

Jenny didn't know what she'd been told and didn't offer any explanation, but it wasn't necessary as after Joan put the kettle on she continued, 'Alexander called us and asked us to take care of the children this evening. He wants to take you out for dinner.'

Amazed, Jenny stood with her mouth open staring at Joan. Then she asked, 'Can you manage — I mean, with William?'

'Cyril thinks William will be tired after his first day back at school, and he will be well occupied with his homework, the cats, and Toby's railway set.'

'I should think he would be,' chuckled Jenny.

So Joan had considered what she was taking on and decided she would be able to cope.

'Cyril is in the garden, measuring

wood for the new shed. I'll give him a shout as I expect he'd like a cup of tea.'

'I'll go and tell him,' Jenny said. 'By the way, in town I bought some pasties for the evening meal so you won't have to worry about feeding the family. And some fish ends for the cat.'

'I've brought some rhubarb from our garden to make a crumble.' Joan took out the long, pink sticks from her shopping basket ready to be chopped up.

'Mmm. They'd probably like custard with that,' Jenny said.

'I know they will!' Joan retorted.

It struck Jenny that Joan and probably Cyril had conspired with Alexander to offer them a night out. It gave her a warm feeling to think that Polly's family now accepted her and wanted to give her a treat.

After making herself a quick sandwich, Jenny went out with it in her hand, munching it as she approached the burned-out shed in the garden.

Soon she was discussing the new

shed construction with Cyril. Where to put it, how to do the foundation work and the design. He seemed to be in his element having this job to do, and Jenny was pleased he was. He'd also brought up his own lawn mower so that the grass could be kept in some sort of order.

'Cyril,' Jenny said with a wry grin, 'would you cut Alexander's hair while you're at it?'

His guffaw sounded so loud that Jenny wondered if Joan would hear it in the kitchen.

'Alexander has a fine mop of hair, not like mine,' Cyril said, stroking his sparse head of hair. 'Combing back his overgrown fringe with his fingers has become a habit with him. I daresay he considers it a gesture that gives him some individual way of appearing to manage the tragedy that has been thrown at him recently.'

Thinking that was probably so, Jenny asked hesitantly, 'Do you think he will . . . recover? I mean, can he cope?'

'Certainly. He has tremendous forti-
tude.'

'Meaning?'

'Just because he hasn't the same bold
personality as his older brother, doesn't
mean he has no courage, grit — whatever you like to call it.'

Jenny took a deep breath.

'Do you think he'll marry again?'

'If the right lady comes along he may
well decide to. But it will be his
decision, and hers. If and when, it
happens.'

Destiny. Jenny was comforted by a
strong feeling that what would be,
would be.

Then picking up his empty cup, she
asked, 'I think I've asked you this
before, Cyril. Will you and Joan mind
. . . I mean, Polly was your beloved
daughter and seeing anyone filling her
place will not be easy for you.'

He gave her a broad smile.

'Don't you worry about that!'

He turned away to get on with his
work. She could understand it must be

painful for him and his wife to have to face that possibility. But he hadn't suggested they would be dead against it, or that they would cut themselves off from Alexander's family if he did. She hoped not. After all, she had helped to bring the family together — especially William and his grandmother.

Walking back towards the house, Jenny was pleased she'd bought her new dress. She would need it for this evening. Most of her clothes, especially her dressier outfits, were still in her flat in London. It seemed as though some guiding hand had pushed her to buy the outfit. She hoped Alexander would like it.

16

Preparing to go out, Jenny was glad she'd bought such a pretty dress and accessories as she'd only managed to stuff a few clothes in a case in a hurry when she went up to her flat in London.

She laid out the dress lovingly and stroked the silkiness of it. The colourful print was joyful, like a sunny day.

As Joan and Cyril prepared for the children to come home, Jenny was able to shower and change for her evening out.

Putting on her lip gloss, she heard the children all coming in at the same time, and then William's voice as he scampered upstairs.

The next thing she knew was a knock at her door and Alexander peering in.

Clearly stunned to see her dressed up, a smile lit up his tired face.

He said almost gruffly, 'I hope you're ready, Jenny. We have a table booked for seven o'clock.'

He glanced meaningfully at the wristwatch she'd given him and she was pleased to recall that it was waterproof, and so had not been harmed as hers had been when she fell into the swimming pool and he rescued her.

Then he closed the door and thundered downstairs.

Perhaps he'd had a bad day at the office? If he had, it wasn't a good start to their evening out. Not, perhaps, the best time to discuss all she wanted to question him about. She sighed.

After a last-minute check in the mirror, Jenny followed him downstairs.

The family were all ensconced in the kitchen with their grandparents. Jenny was glad they were, and she didn't have to listen to any remarks about her being dolled up. All she did was to wish them all a happy evening — as she still hoped to have.

Leaving the house, she was surprised.

Alexander stood by his car holding open the passenger door for her — but his appearance made her blink. He'd had a haircut! Not only that, but he wore what looked like a new suit, fitting his broad shoulders exactly, a silk tie and a fresh striped shirt. So, she wasn't the only one dressed up for the evening!

She gave him a wide smile and said, 'Goodness, Alexander — where on earth are you taking me to eat? Buckingham Palace?'

He grinned.

'Not quite. But I hope it'll be special.'

She gave him a fond look. He'd obviously gone to a lot of trouble to arrange everything, and she felt excited. Restaurant meals were a treat she'd rarely enjoyed in her life, Marvin always having preferred to eat at home.

Having settled her in his new car — which, she was pleased to note, he must have had valeted as it was spotless and seemed even fresher-smelling than when he first got it — Alexander slid into the driver's seat. He drove easily and confidently out into the lane and onto the motorway as though he was now quite used to his superior transport and liked it.

The traffic grew more horrendous the nearer they travelled to London. It was just as well he seemed to know where to go, as she knew she would have been hopeless as a navigator. He was skilled at driving around London, of course, as it was part of his job showing properties.

She didn't like to disturb his concentration so she didn't ask where they were going. She just loved being with him.

★   ★   ★

Their destination was a classy restaurant in the heart of London — one of those ultra-posh eating places Jenny imagined to be frequented by celebrities. She almost protested, wishing he had chosen a less costly venue — a pub or bistro — because of course he would want to pay. It wouldn't be right for her to offer.

Still, he'd booked and she couldn't deny it was great fun to be greeted like royalty by the head waiter, whisked off to a private corner table and to have a large, heavy, folded linen napkin shaken out and laid on her lap.

Of course, she could easily afford to have a meal in a luxury restaurant like this — but until now she had had no handsome male companion to share a table with her. So this was truly special, as Alexander had said it would be.

Her new dress was revealed as she removed her jacket. Alexander's eyes sparkled.

'You look lovely in that dress, Jenny,' he said and her face glowed with pleasure. Normally she was happy enough wearing her jeans and an apron in the kitchen, eating meals straight out of the oven, but today was refreshingly different. She wasn't the cook; she was like the Queen waiting to be served.

'What would you like to drink?' Alexander was obviously used to escorting a guest to a fine restaurant and his confidence rubbed off on her. She was able to relax and enjoy the ambiance.

She was glad of his help reading the menu. It was huge! He ordered drinks so they could spend some time going through the description of each dish until she decided which she would go for.

When the waiter went off with their order, Alexander sighed as he sat back and sipped his non-alcoholic drink.

'So, do you like your new car?' he asked her.

She nodded emphatically. 'Yes, thank you, I do. It's the type I really wanted. Nothing flashy or high-powered — I'm really comfortable with it.'

'Good. I always think it's important to have what you really want. If it's possible.'

She smiled back at him, noting how at ease he now looked.

This was an opportunity to ask him about himself, she realised — to talk in more depth about the issues that affected them both.

So she dived straight in, asking, 'How are you coming to terms with your recent tragedy?'

He looked shocked, and pain flashed across his face. He put down his drink and closed his eyes.

Perhaps that was the wrong thing to have asked? Had she been too direct? She held her breath; she had obviously touched a raw nerve.

After a moment he cleared his throat and said, 'I had to come to terms with it, Jenny. She was killed in a bus accident on a day out. It happened.'

His manner showed he didn't want to discuss it any further, for now at least.

Soft music was playing in the the background.

'I like a bit of jazz,' she said conversationally. How about you?'

His face relaxed. 'I do, actually. Sometimes when the children are in bed I play the kind of music I like.' He rattled off some names of artists that didn't mean much to her. 'Do you?'

Jenny mentioned a few tunes that came into her head. But then the waiter arrived with their starters. The portions were tiny, but rich and full of different flavours.

'How about sport?' she asked.

He mentioned he was keen on badminton and had played it a lot before he got married.

'And I like football,' he added with a smile.

'But now your children take up most of your time, don't they?'

'They do. But I don't regret it. They won't be young for long. I'll be saying goodbye to them in a few years' time as they leave home to work or go to college, I expect.'

Jenny thought that was a very sensible attitude to have. She hadn't thought of the children growing up fast. They wouldn't always be as they were now, needing a lot of care and attention as they grew up.

'You want them to enjoy their childhood, of course,' she said, thinking aloud.

'Of course. I want to enjoy it with them. But I'm so busy, I regret I can't do everything I'd like to.'

Jenny didn't have to be told that. She knew that if she were living with him, it would give him more opportunity for family life.

But she couldn't say that. No, that was one of the reasons for her to hope he might ask her to marry him, because she would enjoy doing family things too. She could take on a lot of the household chores, buy the groceries, take the children to various clubs and parties — indeed, it would be fun. And that would give him time to enjoy his own pursuits, perhaps take William to football matches . . .

'Jenny — you're miles away. The waiter is bringing our main dishes now.'

The food was beautifully cooked and laid out on the plates. She took a few moments to admire the chef's work before she picked up her fork to try the delicious meal.

Their main courses were a feast for the senses that made them both comment delightedly on the dishes they had chosen — in between mouthfuls. They both agreed they had enjoyed their meals.

'Would madam like a dessert?' asked the waiter, offering her a smaller dessert menu.

Madam certainly would! Especially as she anticipated they would be just as delicious as the first courses had been.

Alexander chose the cheese platter, which didn't make her feel she was alone having another course.

It didn't seem to matter that she was aware of a few customers and waiters floating about in the background. They were now fully relaxed and as they sipped their coffee Jenny felt she could ask him personal questions.

'What are your plans for the future, Alexander?'

'Much the same as they are now.'

'Same job?'

'I like what I do. At present, anyway. It gets me out of the office a bit, and looking around and assessing property is interesting. I find selling things suits me.'

She put down her spoon. 'Except when you have awkward clients like me, eh?'

He chuckled. Then he said seriously, 'You're not awkward. You are just waiting for the sun to come out — like me.'

'Well, I think we've missed the sunset tonight — it's dark out there.'

He put his elbows on the table and one hand cupped hers as she replaced the small coffee cup in its saucer.

'Let's go out and see, shall we?'

'Are you by any chance trying to sell me something?' Her eyes caught his.

He laughed as he beckoned the waiter for the bill. 'Wait and see.' He winked at her as he took out his wallet and handed his card to the waiter.

* * *

It was a bit fresh outside, but as Alexander and she wore jackets and walked close together it didn't seem to chill them too much.

He guided her to the embankment by the Thames, which was spectacular by night. There they could stroll and look out over to the Houses of Parliament — which Jenny recognised from the television news. It thrilled her to experience this view and she said so.

Alexander tightened his arm around her body as a sharp gust blew their hair about.

'That's where polititians discuss things,' he said. 'So I thought we might too.'

Jenny felt her heart patter, but said nothing.

He cleared his throat. 'How can I find you a new home if you won't tell me what you are really looking for?'

She stopped walking and looked

down at the leaves scudding around her feet.

'I'm like one of those leaves, Alexander. I feel blown about, at a loss, directionless.'

He seemed irritated. 'I don't think that is true! You are quite capable of making up your mind.'

She snapped back, 'It's all very well for you. You have a home and family.'

'Commitments — yes, I do. But as I explained to you in the restaurant, they won't last a lifetime. My future is as uncertain as yours.'

No, it isn't! Jenny felt hurt for him to think he would soon be in her position. Alone. Then she thought with a slight panic, *Perhaps he will get married again — but not to me.* Many women would find him attractive, desirable, sexy and well off. Her face began to flush as she began to experience the sense of loss she would feel if he did. She'd be truly lost without him around.

'Alexander,' she said, almost shyly, 'will you marry again?'

'I had it in mind.'

'Why?'

He loosened his arm around her shoulders but held onto her hand firmly. 'Because I was married to a lovely woman, and I know how wonderful married life can be if you love someone.'

For a moment or so she took in some air and looked over at the waves dancing in the reflected light on the river.

'The Thames is flowing quite fast,' she found herself saying wistfully.

'Yes,' he agreed. 'Time goes fast. Good times should be enjoyed while you can, Jenny. Before you know it, you'll find yourself drifting into a dull kind of life — instead of having the exhilarating experiences that are yours for the taking.'

Happiness for Jenny seemed like a cloud in the darkened sky. Out of reach. She asked out of curiosity, 'What kind of experiences have you in mind that I should enjoy?'

He put his arm around her again as a crowd of rather noisy young people came along the walkway towards them, singing and shouting.

'Well, to start with, one you've had before. Like this.'

His lips came to cover hers in a lingering kiss. She snuggled against him and kissed him back.

Nestling close to his chest she teased, 'OK, I enjoyed that exhilarating experience. What else?'

He was rubbing the back of her neck with his thumb. 'Let me think. Foreign holidays?'

That sounded wonderfully good. Then the real bugbear came into her mind.

'Luxury resorts would suit me. But who is going to pay for these holiday dreams?'

He seemed taken aback. 'You would!'

She pulled back a little. She'd tried to be generous before and he hadn't liked it had he?

'It wouldn't offend you that I am able to pay?'

'Why should it? Your money is your money. What you decide to spend it on is your affair.'

'But you got so cross when I bought you your car!'

He put his hand under her chin and lifted her face to look at his amused expression.

'Sure, I did. I had arranged for you to have the sports car like the one William sent to the scrap yard — not buy one for me, without even consulting me about what I would like.'

She didn't want to quarrel with him. Not tonight! And yet she had to be bold, be honest about her feelings. Learn what he really thought, too.

So she challenged him saying, 'Fair enough — but you did like it, didn't you?'

'Oh Jenny, when will you understand that a man likes to be boss at times? Some things — your things — are your decision, I respect that. But some are mine. You'll be telling me next what colour to paint my new shed — '

'No, indeed I won't!'

'Well, other family matters then, perhaps. I know what Polly would have liked for her children as they reach adulthood. I would like to make sure I fulfil her wishes if I can. Give her children the upbringing she wanted for them. I know it is rough on you that I am saying this when you have been so kind to them, so understanding and generous.'

The light dawned on Jenny slowly as she gazed into the face of the man she loved. He was not saying he objected to her being rich — or how she spent her money. Only that her money must not lessen his manhood or usurp his right of influence as a father. He didn't want to be obeying her, any more than he expected her to obey him.

She couldn't blame him for that.

Smitten with remorse that she'd behaved so crassly, Jenny felt tears running down her cheeks.

'I've been a bit of an idiot,' she mumbled, trying to find a hankie in her jacket pocket that wasn't there, then trying to locate her handbag to find one in there. But she'd forgotten to bring a hankie and snuffled, 'I'm sorry.'

Alexander was aware that these home truths were painful for her. He hugged her to him and produced his handkerchief for her to use.

When she'd overcome her bout of crying, he kissed her hands and assured her that there was no need for her to be sorry for anything.

'Jenny, ever since I first met you I knew you'd bring sunshine back into my life,' he said. 'And so you do. I owe you so much already. My family love you.'

'As I love them,' she was able to say honestly.

'I want to ask you something,' he broke the short silence that followed, 'but I need you to feel a bit better before I do.'

Some time passed. They walked on with their arms around each other, seeing the river boats bobbing on the water as they floated by. They were aware, too, of people now sheltering under their coats and umbrellas as they hurried by.

The sound of Big Ben, the parliament clock, was just a noise. Neither of them seemed to care one way or another what time it was.

But the wind had whipped up.

'I think we've had enough night air, don't you?'

Jenny agreed. The lively wind was making her ankles feel frozen.

'But before we leave this romantic spot — ' He drew in a deep breath. 'Will you marry me, my Sunshine?'

From despair to ecstasy, those words of his provided immediate balm to Jenny's troubled heart. All of a sudden she knew exactly what she wanted.

'Yes,' she said, with no doubt in her voice.

Now everything seemed clear. She had a home to go to. Not a luxury property, but one she knew she would be content to live in. A happy home with three lively children and a man who wanted her not only as a housekeeper, but as a lover. Their families approved of them. In fact, Alexander went on to reveal that he had asked her father if he approved of the union. Mr Warner had been delighted.

In the years ahead, her role would be mainly as a home-maker. But cooking was her hobby, and she liked working in Polly's kitchen. And having a garden to potter in, to able to grow fresh vegetables, appealed to her greatly.

There would always be people coming in and out of the house; friends to invite and go out and see. She would never be lonely again — as she admitted she had been before she met Alexander.

Then, further in the future, they had a lot to look forward to. Nothing fixed, but with great possibilities for exciting travel experiences.

Their kiss was spontaneous. Their lovemaking would always be that way, Jenny thought, as they hurried out of the wind towards his car.

'We could go to a hotel — just for tonight,' suggested Alexander.

'I haven't brought a nightie,' she protested.

'You won't need one!'

She chuckled, thinking that most good hotels would provide toothpaste and toiletries. Then another problem struck her.

'Who will take William to school tomorrow?'

'This is Friday. No school for a couple of days.'

'But will Joan and Cyril manage, looking after the children until we get back? Won't they expect us to get home?'

'I think Cyril will manage to keep the ship in order until tomorrow — and the ship's cats.'

Jenny laughed, imagining the tussles the grandparents might have when they realised Alexander was not coming home that night. But she knew Joan would put them to bed, as she'd often done since Polly died. And afterwards she could go back home to her own bed — Cyril would walk her there, then come back to the cottage to be on duty overnight. A ship's captain was used to a night shift. And William wouldn't forget to feed his mother's cat. She felt proud to think that she had helped to bring that family together.

'Yes,' she agreed. 'I think they won't begrudge us a night together. They might even prepare the children to be ready to welcome their new step-mother.'

'I hope so.' Alexander's deep voice would always give her thrills. 'Though don't be dismayed if they may see you as their housekeeper for some time. Like cats, they may expect you to feed and wait on them. You may have to be strict with them at times — just as you have been teaching them to clear up after meals and disagreeing about what they may want to do. But soon they will come to see you as part of the family and value your advice.'

'I hope you will allow me to help them financially when they reach their time to fly the nest . . . '

They briefly discussed how they would continue to prevent the children from knowing about Jenny's money until they were older. Until then they would have to learn to spend money wisely and save, if necessary, for what they wanted.

Helping them with student fees and getting on the housing ladder was all way in the future, depending what they and their partners wanted.

Giving to charities was not ruled out. Jenny had a lot of money, but not an endless amount. She wanted to use it with care so that it didn't embarrass her husband or his children.

Her father, too, was not forgotten.

'My dad will be looking for a place to live before long,' she explained.

Alexander talked about his mother and brother too. 'We will have to wait for a couple of years, I expect, before we know what the future holds for them. I would imagine my brother may yet marry — or if he does not, he is the kind of man who likes to work until he has one foot in the grave!'

Jenny nodded. James was such a good surgeon, and his skills would always be needed.

'He will always be welcome at our house,' she said, feeling wonderful to think of the house now as her home.

'You're going to be busy!' remarked Alexander giving her hand a squeeze.

'Yep, I can see that. But it is what I want.'

'Are you quite sure?'

'I'm sure. Are you sure you want me, Alexander?'

He turned to her, his eyes glittering. His passionate kiss was her answer.

So, having talked about their innermost doubts and differences, and settled everything they could think of, their immediate concern was now for practicalities.

Alexander beamed. 'Now shall we see about making our union legal?'

He started the car engine and moved smoothly out of the restaurant car park and into the shopping area, where a number of outlets were still open. He re-parked, leaped out of the car, opened her door and grabbed her hand.

She realised he was taking her to a jeweller and she was not going to be allowed to pay — nor should she offer to pay — for the engagement and wedding rings she chose. Neither did she expect to. That was a groom's prerogative.

She chose the style of ring that she liked, and assured Alexander that she would always wear and treasure her rings.

Should she offer to get him a signet ring? She dismissed the idea — and that of getting herself a new wristwatch. Saying no to ostentatious purchases now, for herself and for others, was going to be necessary. As she had had to do that for most of her life, it wouldn't be a hardship. She was fortunate to have already been on a good spending spree — before she met Alexander.

There were other enjoyable things, many of them free, which she intended to enjoy to the full.

From now on, her life would no longer be one of total freedom to do as she liked. She was going to be in a partnership, experiencing all the highs and lows of married life. She was optimistic it would all be tremendous fun with children and animals around.

Driving through London's theatre-land, they marvelled at the flashing hoarding lights advertising the shows. Seeing the many theatregoers anxious to get to their seats in good time before the curtain went up, Jenny suggested they went to a musical to finish the night off in style.

'OK. It is a special night for us,' Alexander said, nodding in agreement.

The price of the tickets for the popular show, and the charges for the central London underground car parking they found, were eye-watering. Jenny asked him tentatively, 'Shall I pay?'

Alexander replied, 'I think you'd

better — I'm broke!'

She laughed. Holding onto his arm in the queue outside the ticket office she suggested they took the most expensive seats available, and he didn't protest.

Now she was glad she'd won the Lottery! She had the money to pay for their extravagances. From now on, she was looking forward to having some challenges — but also a lot of fun.

After the show, Alexander seemed to have no difficulty finding a cosy hotel just outside the City for them to seal their love for each other — to begin their new life together in harmony.

Jenny knew that their love, based on accepting what had happened earlier in their lives, would see them through the rest of their time together.

⋆　⋆　⋆

Arriving home next day, they were delighted to find that the children had been well-behaved, and their grandparents departed with smiles and kisses.

'Thank goodness they have gone,' declared Katie. 'Now we can bake a wedding cake.'

Alexander and Jenny looked at each other in astonishment.

'How did you know we are planning to get married?' asked Jenny.

'William said that you spent the night together and you wouldn't have unless you intended to marry because you don't when you are here.'

William's face turned a shade as bright as his hair. But he picked up his cat, Belle, and stroked her saying, 'That's OK. We don't object to having a new mother, do we?'

'No,' said Toby, clutching one of his trains. 'Specially if it means we can have some more track and signal boxes and stuff like that.'

'No, you can't!' his father said sternly, turning his glare on Jenny. She just smiled.

'Perhaps at Christmas you may be lucky, Toby.'

'Good, it's not long to wait.' Katie

wanted the final word. 'Jenny and I will be busy until then making mince pies, a Christmas cake and puddings. All the things my mummy used to make.'

There was a chorus of voices. Everyone was talking loudly at once as though they suddenly felt they had a right to say what they felt. Alexander took the opportunity to kiss Jenny and to show the children her sparkling engagement ring.

Then Jenny had to kiss them all for making her so welcome.

When they got the chance to be alone, she received a loving kiss from Alexander.

'No more searching. You are in the right place here, Jenny,' he said softly.